The Stowaway

Also by R.A. Salvatore

The Legend of Drizzt™

R.A. & Geno Salvatore

The Stowaway

STONE OF TYMORA · VOLUME I

MIRRORSTONE

Cover art by Scott Fischer
First Printing: September 2008

9 8 7 6 5 4 3 2 1

ISBN: 978-0-7869-5094-2
620-23960720-001-EN

Cataloging-in-Publication Data is available from the Library of Congress

U.S., CANADA,	EUROPEAN HEADQUARTERS
ASIA, PACIFIC, & LATIN AMERICA	Hasbro UK Ltd
Wizards of the Coast, Inc.	Caswell Way
P.O. Box 707	Newport, Gwent NP9 0YH
Renton, WA 98057-0707	GREAT BRITAIN
+1-800-324-6496	

Please keep this address for your records.

Visit our Web site at **www.mirrorstonebooks.com**

To Mom and Dad
—G.S.

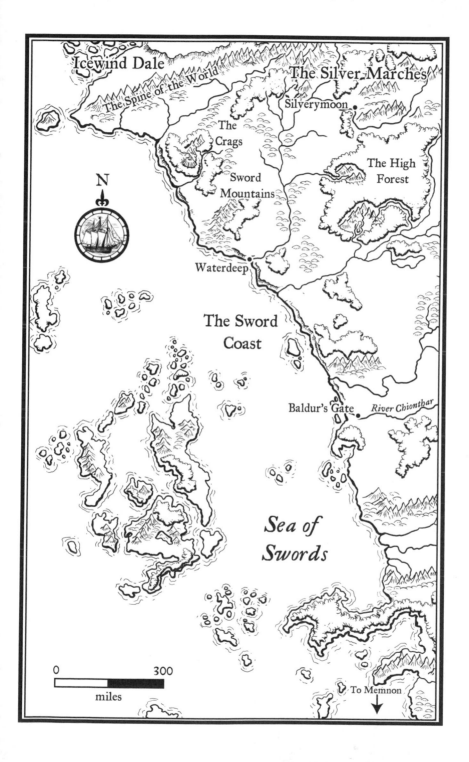

Part One

The Stowaway

The approaching footsteps echoed off the many uneven surfaces of the small cave I lay in. I struggled to sit up, my shoulder sore where I had fallen on it, my wrists raw from the coarse rope tied around them. Flickering light appeared in the wide gap between the warped old wooden door and the stone floor. It was the first light I had seen in several hours.

The door creaked open.

A man stood in the portal, illuminated by the torch he held in his left hand. The light cast shifting shadows across his face, particularly under the brim of his broad black hat. Beneath the hat, a black bandana covered his right eye.

He entered, limping, favoring his left side. I quickly saw the reason: his right leg ended just below the knee, replaced with a weathered wooden peg.

After closing the door behind him, he pulled another torch from a loop on his belt, lit it, then placed the torches in sconces set

3

on either side of the door. The light was still not much, and the shadows danced around the room. But at least I could see.

The old pirate turned toward me, lit ominously from behind, a silhouette, a shadow himself. His hand moved to the cutlass sheathed at his side, and I shuddered.

"Ye're a sailor, aintcha boy?" he said. "Yer skin's known the sea breeze, felt the sun. But it ain't yet leather like mine." He pulled at his many wrinkles, the sea-worn skin stretching in his hand. "But ye're on yer way. So be telling me, sailor-boy, how long ye been on the seas?"

I resisted the urge to answer him. It was the look in his eye. I knew he would kill me. I had been told often that pirates were merciless, bloodthirsty criminals—murderers and thieves—and that to be captured by one was death if there was no one to pay your ransom. I had seen it first hand.

The pirate gave his cutlass a menacing shake and looked right into my eyes. "Ye

R.A. & Geno Salvatore

thought I'd be coming in with me sword drawn and just cut ye down, didn't ye, boy?" he said. "But we could've done that when we took yer ship. Wouldn't have been much use for us to take ye all the way here and cut ye down, would it?"

I shook my head. "I didn't expect you to simply kill me. I expected—I still expect—you to question me first." I swallowed, attempting to still my trembling voice. "But you'll get nothing useful from me."

The pirate slowly drew his sword. "Well then, boy, shouldn't I just be killing ye now? I mean, if ye ain't gonna be giving me nothing *useful*." He burst into a laugh, the sort of laugh heard among friends sitting around a fire, sharing a drink. He slid the sword back into its scabbard. "Now, what be yer name, boy?"

"My name?" I had been prepared for an interrogation. But not for this. I pushed my back against the cave wall and sat up taller. I knew what I had to do.

The Stowaway

"Yer name, boy. It ain't a hard question."
The pirate smiled a crooked smile, showing
as many teeth missing as remaining, several
of them glinting with gold.

"My name does not stand alone," I said,
the tremble gone from my voice. "It comes
with a story. The tale of an artifact—tied to my
soul through no fault or courage or heroism or
hard work of my own. An artifact that has led
me from one adventure to another, leaving a
trail of destruction in its wake."

I stared at the dirty pirate a long while,
forcing my mind down old roads I had tried
to forget.

R.A. & Geno Salvatore

Chapter One

I do not know what name my mother gave me.

I do not know, because every person who knew my name died—killed by a dark creature, a demon called Asbeel—mere days after I first entered the world.

Until I met Perrault, I was an orphan. And ten days after my twelfth birthday, I was alone once again.

Perrault lay unmoving on a bed in an inn. I had gone looking for help, but no help was to be found.

There was only Asbeel.

"Where are you, boy?"

". . . . boy . . . boy . . . boy . . . boy?" His voice echoed off every wall, shaking the timbers of houses all along the streets in that section of the city, shaking the ground beneath my feet. I looked around at the crowded marketplace, expecting to see panic, for how could the people of Baldur's Gate not react to that clamor?

But . . . nothing. Was the voice just for me? Was some demonic magic guiding it to my ears alone?

" . . . boy . . . boy . . . boy . . . boy?"

I couldn't tell where the voice was coming from.

I darted frantically back and forth, looking for some clue, for some place to hide. A man leaning against a tavern door eyed me, thinking me out of my mind, no doubt. And perhaps I was.

The echoes grew louder. " . . . boy . . . boy . . . boy . . . boy!"

I raced down the alley beside the tavern and looked toward the sky. In that instant, all the

R.A. & Geno Salvatore

sound came crashing together and nearly knocked me from my feet.

Asbeel stood a hundred strides away and thirty feet up, and I could see the fires in his eyes and the gleam of his teeth.

I knew—a sensation as heavy as drowning in cold water—that Asbeel had seen me.

I tried to run, but I could not, as if the cobblestones had reached up and grabbed my feet.

Asbeel jumped off the roof, landing in the alleyway with such strength that he hardly bent his legs to absorb the weight of the fall. The buildings shook and the ground trembled, and even the man at the tavern gave a shout, so I knew I was not imagining it.

But how could it be? Asbeel was no larger than an elf, a lithe and sinewy creature who seemed to weigh little more than I did. It made no sense, but nothing did.

The shock of the demon's jump seemed to break away the confining cobblestones, or free me from my own bindings. I knew not which and didn't care. I just turned and ran for all my life.

The Stowaway

Not four steps out of the alleyway, I tripped and fell, skinning both my knees and jarring my wrists. But before I could begin to curse at my clumsiness, a huge crate soared over my head and smashed to pieces in the street in front of me.

I looked back just in time to see Asbeel kick another crate as if it weighed no more than a child's rag-ball. He laughed as it soared out for me, and I could only yelp and fall aside as it shattered precisely where I had been kneeling.

"Hey, now!" the man at the tavern cried, and another came out the door to see what was happening.

My mouth went dry, my heart sank. I wanted to call out to them to run away, to go back inside, but I could not. I hadn't the strength or the courage.

I just ran.

The ground trembled behind me as the beast gave chase. Then the shaking stopped, replaced by screams.

I covered my ears, but could not block out the cries. Not knowing where I was going, I turned every corner I came to, only wanting to be out of Asbeel's sight.

The ground trembled again and I knew he paced me. I ran into one of the main streets and the trembling grew more violent. I could hear his scaly feet slapping the cobblestones. He would grab me at any moment and tear me apart!

I should pull out Perrault's stiletto, I told myself, use its magic to make it a sword, and stab the beast through the heart.

I should . . . I should, I thought, but I could not.

Asbeel's face burned behind my eyes, evil and hideous and hungry, and the thought of it made my legs weak and my heart faint.

As I neared an intersection, a wagon driven by a team of four huge horses veered toward me. I couldn't stop. The driver screamed and tugged the reins with all his might.

The horses, neighing in complaint, barreled past me. I threw myself down and flattened myself between the wheels then managed to get out between the back two just as the driver stopped the cart.

"What, boy? Are ye dead, then?" the driver cried out.

I managed to scream, "No!" as I ran off.

Barely ten strides away, I heard the explosion as Asbeel slammed into the cart. I could picture the wagon shattering, its load of fruits flying wildly. I heard the driver yelp in surprise. I heard the horses whinny in terror and pain.

I peeled around the corner and looked back, just in time to see one of those horses kick Asbeel in the chest, sending him flying backward. He slammed against a wall and stumbled, but did not fall.

I yelled and ran. The demon refocused his anger—I heard more screams.

I turned down another cobbled street, and at last I knew where I was.

I had reached the heart of the temple district of Baldur's Gate. Massive structures all around dwarfed me, churches dedicated to each of the myriad gods of Faerûn, gargoyles and statues gazing down at me, leering or smiling with equal irony and equal uselessness.

The demon's voice rang out again, but it was farther away and full of even greater rage—an echo that would not die.

"You cannot hide, boy," the voice said. "Fall down and let yourself be taken."

But beneath his voice rang another, a woman's, perfect and clear as a clarion in the fog. It was but a whisper, but I could hear it distinctly.

Run now, and take heart.

Despite the clutch in my chest and the pain in my knees, the woman's voice compelled me.

I sprinted toward the sun that descended over the cityscape. The voices in my head grew fainter, and I felt less of the fear that had nearly crippled me. I felt myself coming under my own control again, aware of my surroundings. I slowed my pace.

As I tried to catch my breath, the leather bandolier I hid beneath my shirt dug into my shoulder, as if it were made of thick chains and not leather. In a pouch on that leather bandolier

The Stowaway

was a stone, dark as night and heavier than its small size suggested.

It had been in my possession for only ten days—a gift from Perrault—and already it had brought more grief than I had known possible. It had brought ruin to everyone I knew. And if I could not find a way to escape Asbeel, it would bring about my ruin too.

I glanced up and down the crooked street. The shadows grew longer; soon darkness would fall. I didn't want to be out alone, at night. And I didn't want to face Asbeel, alone, in the dark.

But where could I go? I thought of returning to the Empty Flagon, the inn where I had left Perrault only a few hours ago. By then the tavern would surely be full of patrons. The proprietor, a crazy old dwarf named Alviss, would be floating behind the bar and around the room on one of his flying blue discs. Flagons of mead would drift of their own accord out to thirsty customers then return, emptied, and with the coin paid.

And in the room at the back of the tavern, I would find Perrault, lying in bed. For a moment,

14

I imagined I could race back to the inn, speak the password, enter the place, and have Perrault tell me what I should do. But Asbeel would surely come to look for me at the Empty Flagon. And I did not know the city well enough to find another place to hide. I had no other choice. I had to leave Baldur's Gate without him. The only question was how.

From the high hill of the temple district where I stood, I saw the whole sweeping descent of the bustling port and the long wharf at its end. The last of the day's vessels were just sailing up toward the city. I watched as one cut down the river, the small flag atop its mainmast fluttering in the wind. The weight lifted from my chest.

And a plan formed in my head.

The Stowaway

Chapter Two

I snuck through the inner city and made my way to the river where I waited for morning to come. Nestled in a pile of crates at the end of the city's long wharf, I stayed awake all through the night. My heart raced at every sound, certain Asbeel had discovered me.

At last the sun rose and I felt safe enough to creep out of my hiding place. Many of the ships I had seen at anchor the previous evening were gone, having sailed out at first light. Those that remained had a steady stream of crew returning.

I would have to play a waiting game.

The wind was strong and blew directly out to sea from the east, where the sun was rising. The air was warm despite the wind, and it felt good across my face.

I was sure no ships would be coming in against such a headwind, so to execute my plan, I had to pick one already docked. It would be a good day for departures, and I was sure most of the ships would be putting out before the breeze turned. All I needed to do was decide which one to hide aboard.

I moved along the wharf toward the city, and something caught my eye. Sure enough, a ship sailed upriver against the current and the blowing wind, tacking mightily and smoothly, cutting from side to side as if a ship were meant to sail like that, always like that, only like that.

I watched for some time, mesmerized, as the lone ship made its way toward the city. After a while, a small crowd began trotting along the docks. Several guards in uniform and a chubby man with a small stack of papers—the harbormaster,

R.A. & Geno Salvatore

I guessed—prepared to record the new arrival. Then I realized they were gathering at the foot of the wharf I was sitting on.

I crouched behind one of the crates lining the wharf and prayed they hadn't seen me.

The ship stopped her tack and dropped sail, slowly gliding in along the dock. Her name, *Sea Sprite,* was painted in graceful though fading letters along her bow, and she was everything I was not looking for: small and sleek, in perfect condition, looking like the perfect craft for open water.

On her foredeck stood a human in very fine dress—the captain, I supposed. Next to him loomed a giant of a man, huge and imposing with long golden hair that shone in the morning sun. Beside him stood an unusual elf.

My gaze fixed on the elf. Something was not quite right about him, about the way he carried himself. He looked like a typical sun elf, with golden skin and light brown hair, but didn't seem comfortable in that skin. For a moment, it occurred to me that he was another of Asbeel's heritage, and I nearly ran away.

The Stowaway

When he turned to look in my direction—to look at me, I realized, despite my hiding place—I recognized that discomfort again in his striking lavender eyes. That elf was different, I realized, and I felt the fool for thinking him connected to that beastly demon.

The ship was just putting in and would likely not put back out for a tenday. She was well cared for, and I figured that to mean an attentive captain and crew. She was small, with fewer places to hide than a great galleon. Every logical reason told me to pick a different ship.

But the elf intrigued me.

I decided right then and there that I would stow away aboard that ship. All her faults—which were really virtues—were outweighed by the look in the strange elf's eyes.

"What ho, *Sea Sprite?*" the harbormaster called to the captain. "Is Deudermont at your reins?"

The man in captain's garb called back. "He is! And glad to see Pellman, as well!"

Pellman, the harbormaster, had the look of a sailor, his skin leathered by the salt breeze, but his

R.A. & Geno Salvatore

form spoke of a more sedentary lifestyle. Idling about the docks keeping his records, he probably took ample food from the various trading ships as they made berth, enough food certainly to keep his large belly full.

"Well met, Captain," the chubby man called. "And as fine a pull as I've ever seen! How long are you in port?"

"Two days, then off to the sea and the south," Deudermont replied.

Pellman called again. "I seek two adventurers—might you have seen them? Drizzt Do'Urden and Wulfgar by name, though they may be using others. One's small and mysterious—elflike—and the other's a giant and as strong as any man alive!"

Deudermont turned to his two companions, who were hidden from the harbormaster's view, and spoke briefly with them before calling down his answer. " 'Twas Wulfgar, strong as any man alive, who made the pull!" As he spoke, Wulfgar then the elf—Drizzt Do'Urden—stepped forward, showing themselves to Pellman.

The Stowaway

That gave me a name for those violet eyes, and a name for the ship, and she was leaving in two days. Perfect.

The ship tied off quickly, smoothly, the crew executing its task to perfection. *Sea Sprite* had a shallow draw, and so was tied up close to the wharf. I saw my opportunity. Tied to the back of the ship was a launch, a two-person craft with oars, used to go ashore where there was no pier. The boat was tied to the back of the ship through a pair of small holes, too small for a man to crawl through.

Too small for a man, but not too small for me.

I watched as the crew disembarked and began loading supplies. I crouched in my hiding spot, hoping to catch a glimpse of Drizzt, but he was lost among the dockworkers. Wulfgar, the man I thought must have giant blood in him, helped from the deck, but never set foot off the ship. Midday passed, and before I knew it, the sun was moving into the western sky. With the day's work finished, many of the crew left the docks and headed for the taverns. A few guards took positions along the rails of the ship to keep watch.

R.A. & Geno Salvatore

I waited for the guard stationed on the aft deck to move to the far rail, then I quickly dashed forward. When he returned to the aft rail, I was almost directly below him. But he was expecting no trouble, and hardly even glanced in my direction. As he moved away, I began the more difficult part of the task.

The side of the ship was slick, even above the waterline, and the boards were fitted tightly together, but I managed to find small handholds to pull myself up. I climbed a few feet then sidled along the back of the ship until I was alongside the rowboat. My fingertips ached from the strain of holding myself, and I felt more than a few splinters dig in, but I would not let go. That ship was my freedom, and I saw only one way aboard.

The launch hung from ropes and dangled perhaps three feet behind the ship. I could climb no higher—the hull sloped outward, and I could see no more handholds. I would have to take a chance.

I pulled my legs up to my chest and braced them against the ship's hull. I took a deep, steadying

The Stowaway

breath, then let go with my hands and kicked out with my legs. I turned in midair, reaching for the launch. My hands made contact with the side of the ship . . .

And I slipped.

I lost my hold on the little boat, my only hope of getting aboard that ship. As I plummeted toward the water, I reached out in desperation, trying to grab the launch, the ship, anything.

My hand hit something solid, and I clutched at it.

It was neither the ship nor the boat, but one of the two ropes meant for securing the smaller boat. It had come untied—how, I do not know, for sailors' knots never come undone when they aren't supposed to—and the line had dropped right beside me.

The rope scoured my palm as I slid down it. But I held on with all my might, refusing to let go.

The launch swayed dangerously, and I thought it might tumble from its position—if one knot could come untied, the other could as well, as could the rope dangling from the aft deck. After a few moments I stopped swinging so wildly, and slowly pulled myself up the rope and onto the launch, my hands burning the whole time.

When I reached the launch, I realized my luck was even better than I had first thought. My plan had been to squeeze through one of the holes where the ropes tied the launch to the hull. Up close, I saw I could fit through the hole, but not with the rope threaded through the space. With a rope untied, one hole lay empty and I could pull myself through, bringing the rope with me. I tied it off, trying to duplicate the knot on the other rope. At last, the launch was secure enough, I was inside the hold of *Sea Sprite,* and no one was coming to investigate. I breathed a sigh of relief—breathed it into my aching hands, trying to soothe the pain—and moved some barrels to find a spot to settle in for the night.

The Stowaway

Chapter Three

I spent the next two days exploring the space I had claimed for myself. When there weren't sailors in the hold, I roamed around, finding barrels of dried fruit and jerky and filching enough to eat, but only a little from each barrel so it wouldn't be noticed.

I couldn't have picked a better place to stow away. I was far aft, away from the main hatch to the hold, and the containers were piled high. All the new cargo, mostly food, was stored near the bow of the ship. Back near the stern I found mostly trade goods, which wouldn't be unloaded until we reached a port, and with luck, not until I had safely made my getaway.

The goods were exotic and interesting— a barrel of a rare black spice, ground into fine powder; boxes of an ivorylike substance carved into various shapes; and crate upon crate of salt.

During those two days in port, I tried to turn my thoughts away from Perrault and what had become of him at the inn. But at night, he haunted my dreams. I tossed and turned in my makeshift bed, one nightmare after another startling me awake. I longed to go up on deck to count the stars like Perrault had taught me when I was six years old and couldn't sleep. It was the only way I knew to find peace, but I dared not leave the hold. And so I stayed, day and night, praying for time to pass quickly until the ship headed out to sea.

At first the solitude was nearly unbearable, but then I found a single barrel of ceramic marbles, each about the size of the knuckle of my thumb. Those marbles became my only amusement. I rolled them around, watching them move with the sway of the ship. I juggled them, tossing three or even four into the air, catching each as it fell then tossing it up again as the next came down. I even played with some of the rats on the ship, trying to roll a marble into a rat before it saw what was coming and darted away. I never actually hit one, but the game kept my mind occupied.

The third day, I awoke to much clamor from above, and to a great swaying of the ship. I darted to the rope holes, my only view to the outside world, and looked out to see Baldur's Gate receding into the distance.

Behind the city, the sun rose looking larger than I had ever seen it. The sun seemed to cover the entire city, that huge city I had been so impressed with when first I looked upon it. I stared into that beautiful sunrise, but I couldn't help but see darkness beneath it. The city faded behind me, and with it faded Perrault.

Down the Chionthar River we sailed, angling to port, to the south, almost as soon as we crossed the mouth of the river into the open ocean. The coast was in view, behind and to our left, for a good long way as we ran tight and parallel. As the sun moved to the west, we turned again, heading to the open ocean. I did nothing but watch the sea that day, not even thinking to play with the marbles and the rats.

I stayed hidden all day, waiting until the crew had gone to their crowded bunks on the deck above the hold. When night fell, I crept stealthily to the top deck.

I figured if anyone caught me out at sea, there was little they could do. Perhaps they would make me scrub pots in the galley, or swab the deck endlessly, or suffer at some other disgusting task. But they could not throw me off the ship—could they? Surely they wouldn't murder me. They were merchant sailors, not pirates.

Silent as a shadow, I stepped out under a sky filled with stars. The gentle ocean breeze welcomed me from my prison, and the air, which had smelled salty even below decks, burned in my nostrils with the brine of the sea.

Sailors were posted here and there, and though they weren't particularly attentive, I was careful to

R.A. & Geno Salvatore

avoid them. I had decided that there was only one place to spend the night: the crow's nest.

As I made my way to the railing, I reached under my shirt and gripped the bandolier binding my chest. In only a moment, I would be rid of the cursed stone once and for all. I would throw it into the ocean and never think of it again. But as I opened the pouch that hid the stone, I hesitated. All I saw was Perrault, his face stern but his eyes smiling. I saw him in my head, and I felt him in my heart. But I also felt the weight of the stone, the weight of my guilt. And it was more than I could bear.

"Dangerous for a stowaway to be on deck, isn't it?" came a whispering voice.

I nearly yelped aloud. Such a scream would have alerted the other sailors, so I stifled it. I quickly closed the pouch, rearranged my shirt, and turned to face my discoverer.

He was hidden in shadow just beyond the mast, his form indistinct. All I could see were two points of burning lavender flame, the eyes of the elf, Drizzt Do'Urden.

The Stowaway

"What are they going to do to me?" I whispered. I tried to seem confident, defiant even, but somehow the words only sounded scared.

"That depends," replied Drizzt, "on whether they catch you. But if they do, Captain Deudermont would be well within the law to throw you to the sharks."

I stammered, trying in vain to answer, but nothing intelligible came out.

The elf smiled. At least, his eyes brightened, so I assumed he was smiling, though I could not make out his facial features.

"But he seems an honorable man to me," the elf continued, "and would more likely put you to work. But that depends on whether or not they catch you."

"You aren't going to turn me in?" I asked.

He shook his head. "I'm a passenger, same as you. Well, perhaps not quite, since my passage is paid. But I have neither need nor desire to give you away. I would ask one question of you, though. Why do you risk so much to come out on deck?"

R.A. & Geno Salvatore

It was my turn to smile, in relief. "I can't see the stars from the hold." It wasn't a lie.

Drizzt looked at me for a long moment then gave a slight nod. "The stars are worth such a risk, indeed."

"Yes, sir, they are."

"Then I shall leave you to them." He turned and walked away before I could reply.

I made my way carefully, quietly, to the main-mast, looking over my shoulder, certain I would find the elf watching me. When I reached the simple ladder of metal pegs, I put my foot on the first rung and began to climb.

The view was as incredible as I'd hoped it would be, a clear sky stretching infinitely in all directions. The stars twinkled and blinked, and their reflections sparkled on the sea, and I could not tell where the sky stopped and the ocean began.

A cool breeze washed over my face and I took a deep breath, drinking in the salty smell of the sea. Perhaps it was something Drizzt had said, or perhaps it was just that spectacular view stretching

The Stowaway

before me, but the stone and Asbeel no longer weighed so heavily on my mind.

I shouldn't risk tossing the stone here, I decided. The time wasn't right. It could be too easily found again. Instead I would hide aboard the ship and sail to the ends of Toril—or as far as *Sea Sprite* could take me, and when I could sail no farther, then I would drop the thing into the ocean. And I would start my life again.

I wished I could spend the entire voyage in the crow's nest, but I knew that if I did, I would surely be discovered. And after what Drizzt had told me, I dared not take that chance.

I stayed in the crow's nest the whole of the night, though, only climbing down when the eastern horizon began to glow with predawn light. The crew was stirring as I slipped by, but no one took notice of me and I reached my hiding spot undetected. I was soon dreaming again, seeing Perrault, but the dreams were pleasant and warm.

I spent the next two days in a similar routine: sleeping during the day, and climbing to the crow's nest at night.

R.A. & Geno Salvatore

On our fourth day out from Baldur's Gate, something woke me.

It took me a long while to get my bearings, to realize what had stirred me from my sleep. I was still below, and no one had found me, but a great commotion took hold above as sailors rushed to and fro, shouting and yelling. Most of their words were lost to me, but one word, shouted over and over, told me everything.

"Pirates!"

The Stowaway

Chapter Four

My heart dropped. Pirates! If they took the ship, they would loot the hold, and my hiding spot would be compromised. If pirates took me, they would not be so lenient as the elf had been a few nights earlier. They would throw me to the sharks, or keelhaul me, or worse.

I steadied myself. They would not take the ship, I thought, not with the elf and the giant aboard. And if they did, they would not take me easily. I would go down swinging.

I drew my dagger—Perrault's dagger—and

rolled it in my hand, feeling its balance, its magic, its power. I had seen Perrault use its magic before: a simple flick of the wrist would extend it into a fine sword. I knew how to wield such a blade, and though I had never been in real combat, I was confident of my ability to defeat any drunken pirate.

If more than one pirate came, I would hold them off as long as I could. That corner of the hold was my kingdom, my little patch of the world, and it would not fall, no matter the foe. I would rather die than be taken by pirates.

But my determination died as *Sea Sprite* tried to evade her pursuers. A battle at sea is not like a battle on land, where armies line up and charge at each other, and the victor is usually the army that can bring the greatest numbers to the battle most quickly. On the sea, the battle is won or lost by positioning, by eliminating threats one at a time. *Sea Sprite* was a sleek and speedy vessel. I hoped the ships chasing her were not.

As *Sea Sprite* rolled, breaking through the swells, I thought about Captain Deudermont's tactics. The pirates would try to prevent his escape, while

R.A. & Geno Salvatore

Captain Deudermont would try to get out of the pirates' range, so that he may face them individually. On the great expanse of the Sea of Swords, that probably meant hours of sailing before the first arrows were fired.

I peered out the holes in the stern, but saw nothing but open sea. With a heavy sigh, I settled myself down for an agonizing wait. I began tossing marbles, trying to bounce them off the crates and back to my hand without moving my wrist. I had become quite good at that game, and the repetition put me into something of a trance.

Without warning, I was thrown from my reverie.

I say "thrown," because I found myself suddenly in midair. The ship cut a turn, the sharpest turn I ever imagined any ship cutting. *Sea Sprite* cut so sharply that her bow lifted clear out of the water and she pivoted on her stern. The sudden move sent all the barrels and crates in the hold—as well as me—tossing and tumbling, head over heels and end over end, to bump and bang against each other. A cask of water burst, a barrel of salt

The Stowaway

spilled open, and a box of carved ivory slammed into the wall barely an inch from my head. With a crushing, grinding noise, the ship settled down as quickly as it had lifted.

Above decks, the hoots of victory and cries of rage turned to steel clashing against steel, shouts of pain, and the stomp of many, many boots across the deck. My blood raced, and I gripped my dagger, ready to stab any enemy who dared approach. But for the time being, no one entered the hold, and the waiting became unbearable.

I decided to peek at the action through the holes in the stern. I stuck my head out just enough to see that we were entangled with a larger ship.

In the distance, a ball of fire arced off the hull of another ship. As soon as the ball cut through the air, I realized what it was: burning tar, launched by a catapult and headed directly for *Sea Sprite*. Headed directly for the stern of the ship. Headed directly for . . . me!

I ducked.

I heard no crash of the missile against the hull, so I poked my head up to look. Directly below me, the water churned and I watched with great relief as the last lick of flames sank beneath the waves.

Another ball of fire soared over the other ship, but it didn't arc toward us—it didn't arc at all. My breath caught in my throat. What was it? Was it a dragon? Was it some powerful spell? If a wizard had thrown such a fireball, that wizard must be as a god, for it seemed as though one of the stars had dropped out of the sky.

Orange flames rent the cloudless blue. Sky and sea appeared as a painting, with a great fire roaring behind it, and someone tearing a jagged rip across that painting to reveal the flames.

I soon realized that the flames had a shape. It was no fireball or dragon—it was a chariot of fire, horses and carriage ablaze!

I lost my breath as the fiery thing cut sharply around *Sea Sprite* then soared toward the second pirate ship with purpose. The chariot plunged right through the pirates' mainsail, lighting the canvas on fire.

Then a silver streak blazed toward the ship from the chariot. A woman on the back of the flying craft fired a bow. Another bolt of silver leapt out. The catapult strained to respond, but its shot barely lifted into the air then it dropped back onto the deck of the ship.

I couldn't take my eyes off the spectacle. My heart raced as the chariot raced, and leaped as it cut graceful turns, and I nearly cried out when I spotted the driver—a red-bearded dwarf, hollering as if he were truly enjoying the wild ride. The chariot whipped around again, clipping the top of the pirate mainmast, lighting it like a candle. Then the flaming craft turned, moving toward us.

Something dropped off the back of the chariot—the woman archer, I guessed, had abandoned her ride. I leaned out, trying to see where she had splashed down, and to see where the chariot was headed.

I held my breath at the sight of a third pirate ship approaching. I prayed that the chariot would similarly cripple it.

But the chariot did better than that. I heard a cry for Moradin, a dwarf god, and that crazy

R.A. & Geno Salvatore

driver steered the chariot right onto the deck of the third pirate vessel. If all the wizards of Baldur's Gate had lined up side by side and hit the ship with a fireball, it would not have been as grand an explosion! The sight of it stole my breath, then the brightness of it stole my sight.

I fell back and spent a moment blinking. As soon as I could see, I returned to my portal, not wanting to miss the incredible battle.

But then a scaly green hand, its long fingers ending in sharp, filthy claws, hooked over the hole right in front of my face.

Chapter Five

I fell back and lashed out with my dagger, more on instinct than thought. My blade bit deep into the monster's hand, severing a finger. The hand withdrew, but didn't loosen its grip—it ripped a few planks out of the hull as it fell back.

I stared out the now-massive hole in the hull, hoping to watch the beast splash into the sea below.

But instead I saw it dangling from the launch by one hand. It would have been nine feet tall if it were standing, and its arms were long even for its body. It glared up at me, and its hideous pointed nose and crooked teeth would have been enough to unsettle the hardiest of soldiers—and I was no soldier! I looked into its murderous eyes and I felt as if my heart had stopped.

My mind cried out to stab it, to attack, to kill it while it hung from the rowboat. But my body would not answer that call. All I could do was retreat a few steps as the thing ripped at the hull, pulling planks off with ease. When the hole was large enough, it swung itself through.

A surge of fear snapped me from my stupor, and I took the only action I could think of.

I turned and ran.

I hoped my small size would help me. I was able to navigate through the tight spaces of the hold easily, and the hulking thing surely could not. I realized my error as the first few boxes went soaring over my head.

"Come out, tasssty snack," the thing gurgled. Its voice was something between a roaring bear and a drowning cat, every bit as ugly as the monster itself.

R.A. & Geno Salvatore

I picked my way through the familiar cask maze, toward the hatch to the deck, to anywhere the beast was not. But the ship's sharp turn and the crash had tossed the contents of the hold, and I could barely keep my footing.

The troll tossed another barrel at my head, and it crashed among several casks of water, one of which burst open. Other crates and boxes tumbled about.

One of the crates, full of dried and salted meat, landed directly on me, knocking me down and blasting the breath from my lungs. The troll ripped through the last stack of barrels right behind me.

"Oh—ho! Cannot hide!" the brute shouted in delight. Then it stopped abruptly, and when I dared to glance back, it stood staring at me.

It stared at my chest, where my shirt had been torn open. Stared at the sash holding the black stone.

"Ohhh, the demon wantsss it, don't it be?" Its voice was a shrill whisper, like a nail pulled across glass. "'E'll pay me well, won't 'e, then?"

The Stowaway

I snapped my wrist out, extending the magical blade, and swung as hard as I could. But the creature was quicker than I thought, and it stepped out of my reach.

"Eet hasss bite, eet does!" snarled the troll in a strange half-laugh. "But so does I!"

It lunged forward.

I dodged to my left and cut a quick backhand with my saber, aiming to hit the creature in the ear, or at least force it back.

But the beast caught my arm in its hand.

In desperation, I reached my other hand into the nearest barrel and grabbed a handful of powder. Without thinking, I hurled the white stuff into the beast's ugly face.

The sea-green thing howled but didn't loosen its grip on my forearm. "Sssalt!" it shrieked. "The tasssty snack attacks with salt! Oh ho! I leeve in the sea, foolish thing. Salt is my friend, is not yours."

At least it wasn't eating me as it spoke, I thought, reaching into the next barrel. Again, only powder, but I threw it in the troll's face, hoping to buy some time.

RA. & Geno Salvatore

But this time the powder was black—it was pepper imported from the town of Nesmé, that rare spice I had found when I first came aboard. The creature yelped in pain.

It released my hand and grasped at its face with its filthy claws. I grabbed another handful and ran between its massive legs, heading toward the wall through the path the brute had just cleared, a plan forming in my head.

I pocketed the spice as I approached the gaping hole in the hull. Quickly I scanned the nearby barrels to be sure everything I needed was still there, popping open a barrel and a box. Then I went to the hole, using my sword to pull the dangling rope back onto the ship. Perrault's sword was a good one, and I quickly cut the other rope tying the launch to the hull, allowing the small craft to swing freely from the overhead rope.

Heavy footsteps thumped behind me like the beating of my own heart. I had no time!

I turned and grabbed three small objects from the open box—the ivory carvings.

49

Quickly I put them up into the air in a graceful juggle.

"Hey, you," I called to the monster. "If you don't eat me, I'll give you these!"

"Oh ho, the tasssty snack does not want to be snack, does it then? Eet bribes me! But no, I thinksss, I want the snack. Sailing is hungry work, so eet ees." The thing stopped, deep in thought—as deep as such a creature was capable of, I figured. It spoke again. "I can take the treenkets from eets corpse, can't I?" It moved forward again.

I tossed one of the pieces toward the beast, yelling, "Catch!"

Sure enough, the dim-witted troll glanced up at the flying object—not for long, but long enough. I pegged off the other two pieces, hitting the thing right between the eyes with both. But it hardly felt the blows.

It roared and charged.

I grabbed the open barrel and tipped its contents—hundreds of tiny ceramic marbles—directly into the wretch's path.

R.A. & Geno Salvatore

The monster slipped and fell, crashing heavily into the wall beside the gaping hole.

I did not wait. As soon as the barrel fell, I grabbed the loose rope and swung myself out toward the launch, climbing as fast as I could, hand over hand, up onto the small boat. The creature oriented itself quickly and appeared at the hole, snarling in rage.

"You die now." Its voice, that unearthly gurgle, was lower in pitch and more intense. Even several feet away, I could feel and smell its horrid breath.

The creature reached at me with its long arms and grabbed the side of the launch. Slowly, it began to pull the boat nearer.

I could have cut at those hands with my saber, but I knew I would not dislodge the thing. Instead, I grabbed the rope still attached to the launch and began to climb.

"You not escape," the troll promised, pulling harder, trying to bring the launch close enough to grab me before I got away. It leaned out of the ship, its foul breath billowing at me, its teeth gnashing hungrily. It leaned, and it pulled . . .

I gripped the rope more tightly with my left hand and swung my sword with my right, cutting the rope just about where my knees dangled.

Off balance, and suddenly burdened with the weight of the boat while leaning too far forward, the troll toppled and fell. It reached up to swat at me, but the strike had no strength and its claws did not dig in.

Down fell the launch and the wretched beast along with it. The boat landed with a splash, and the troll landed atop it, smashing right through, reducing the rowboat to flotsam. The ripples looked an awful lot like those created by the ball of pitch, in precisely the same spot.

The troll's strike had caused me to swing, and suddenly I was veering back toward the ship, toward the hole where the troll had ripped planks out of the vessel. I saw the sharp edges of broken wood rising up to meet me even as I fell, but I felt the pain of it gashing my chest for only a moment.

Then I felt no more.

Chapter Six

When I awoke, I felt as if I were gently stepping out of a dream. In fact, I thought I was still dreaming.

A most beautiful face hovered over me. Her eyes were the deepest, purest blue, and they smiled sadly at me, comforting me despite the burning pain in my chest. Her red-brown hair flowed over her shoulders, wet but still perfect.

Looking at her, I recalled the fiery chariot, its archer diving out right before it crashed into the pirate ship . . .

So that is why we won, I thought: The gods sent us an angel.

"Who . . . are . . . ?" My throat was so parched the words burned as spoke. I coughed, and pain seared my shoulder and my chest.

"Rest, child." The woman stroked my forehead until the coughing eased. "My name is Cattibrie. Everything is all right now."

I looked up to see the door opening. Three forms silhouetted against the incoming light—a dwarf, an elf, and a giant of a man.

My eyes fell on the middle figure, on Drizzt Do'Urden, his lavender eyes burning with intensity. His skin appeared black in the dim light, I realized, and it was no trick.

I had heard of dark elves before, of the drow who lived beneath the world. They were the subject of many nighttime stories, bogeymen who came out in the darkness to raid elven villages and kidnap babies.

But I was not afraid of that elf, that drow. He had not turned me in to the captain when he'd had the chance. He understood what a night spent staring at the stars might mean to someone like me. In the brief time we'd spoken, I sensed no malice, only sympathy. For whatever reason, he had chosen to protect me.

Drizzt stepped toward my bed, hesitation in his step. "How is he?" he asked in a low voice.

I remembered the first time I laid eyes upon the elf, when he had appeared as a surface elf but had looked so uncomfortable in his own skin. I suddenly understood why. He had been wearing some sort of magical disguise. And it was gone. Now that he could be himself, the discomfort I sensed was gone, too.

Catti-brie looked at the elf and his two companions. "I'm sure the boy appreciates your concern, but ye three are no help here." She waved them away and turned to me. "Ye all be going, now. I'll just be holdin' this one's hand a bit, while they take care of him." She nodded past me, and I followed her gaze to a pair of men entering the room. They carried a small bucket, steam rising off the top.

I tried to mumble something, to ask what was

happening, what they were doing, but I could not produce anything intelligible.

I heard the door shut, and I felt her hand holding mine, strong and callused yet soft. The men set down the bucket—it was filled with black liquid, and I could feel the heat pouring off it. One of the men took up a large metal spoon.

Catti-brie whispered something under her breath—a prayer, I thought—and the man lifted the spoon up to my wounded shoulder.

Suddenly the pain worsened tenfold, a hundredfold. I tried to scream but there was no air in my lungs. I tried to focus on those blue eyes, but there was too much water, more tears than I knew I had. The pain was too intense and I passed out.

Some time later, I awoke. "The tar cauterizes the wound," said a voice—a man's voice.

"Cauterizes?" I mumbled, not even opening my eyes.

R.A. & Geno Salvatore

"It burns the flesh together, so the wound won't bleed."

"Sounds painful." I would have laughed if it didn't hurt so much.

"I've been told it is. But it's better than the alternative." The man's voice was firm, but not unkind.

"What is the alternative?" I was mumbling so badly, I could hardly believe the man could understand me.

"Bleeding to death. And that is no way for a lucky child like you to die."

At the words "lucky child" I opened my eyes, hopeful. But the man standing before me was unfamiliar—or, rather, I had never met him. He wore a regal, if threadbare, blue uniform, and he spoke clearly, with great dignity.

"I am Captain Deudermont of *Sea Sprite,* and you are unlawfully aboard my ship," he said.

Great, I thought. I save his ship from that troll and he's going to toss me overboard?

"I'm very sorry, sir," I said. "But I have an explanation. You see, what I am—"

"What you are, young sir, is a stowaway, and a thief," the captain spat.

In spite of my throbbing shoulder, I sat up. I tried to respond but the captain held out his hand.

"What you are not," Deudermont continued, "is a coward."

I perked up—that hardly sounded like a bad thing.

"Can you take orders?" he asked.

I blinked a few times before answering. "Yes, sir."

"Can you show dignity and bravery in the face of danger?"

"Yes, sir."

"Can you be loyal to those around you, peers as well as superiors?"

"Oh, yes, sir, I can, sir."

"Then, young man, I think I can find a place for you on my ship. If you so desire." For the first time, Captain Deudermont smiled— not a wide smile, but a dignified smile. And it was enough.

I started to respond, but he cut me off. "Do

R.A. & Geno Salvatore

not answer right now. You have many days of healing before you could be useful, anyway. We shall care for you until you're fit, and then you can give your answer."

He turned to leave.

"Wait! Sir!" I called with as much force as I could.

He turned back. "Yes, young man?"

"My name is Maimun. You . . . you never asked my name."

Part Two

The Stowaway

"Took yerself long enough to get to the point!" the old pirate said with a chuckle.

"Exactly long enough," I answered.

"Gave yer name ter Deudermont pretty danged quick. Yer thinkin' he's better'n me, more deservin' yer name? More deservin' yer respect?"

"He didn't ask. You did. I do not reward greed."

The chuckle turned into a laugh. "Some'd say, greed be its own reward!"

"They'd be wrong."

"I'd expect you to say that, fool boy." In the blink of an eye his laugh was gone, his face a profound scowl. With surprising grace for a one-legged old man, he rose to his feet and snapped his cutlass from its sheath. "Ye learned from Deudermont, righteous old fart that he is."

"I learned much from Captain Deudermont," I answered indignantly. "He is a good man, one of many I've known, and all of them far better than you."

The Stowaway

"Don't ye know better'n to insult a man holding a sword?" He brandished his blade but made no move to strike.

I waited, staring into that scowl, goading him with my eyes, challenging him to take the swing. But the cutlass did not fall.

"Well, perhaps yer captain'll pay yer ransom then. And my *greed,*" he practically spat the word, as if it were distasteful to speak, "will be rewarded." He turned as if to leave, taking one of the torches from its sconce.

"Deudermont is not my captain," I said. "And he would not pay pirate ransom even if he were."

The old man stopped in his tracks and turned slowly toward me. "Yerself better start speakin' again, and ye better start speakin' fast, else I'll cut yer head from yer shoulders."

"Perhaps. But I have a question for you. What is *your* name?"

"Ye haven't earned enough of my respect to know it," he spat. "Now talk. Tell me of

R.A. & Geno Salvatore

this artifact. Where did ye get it, and where is it? We ain't found it on ye when we pulled ye from the drink."

"You want the artifact?" I said. "Well, then, you should know its whole bloody story."

Chapter Seven

I know nothing of my birth. I know nothing of my parents, siblings, neighbors. I do not know what day I was born, nor the name or location of my first home.

I do not know because when I was an infant, raiders attacked my hometown. They burned all the buildings, and killed all the people.

Somehow, I survived.

My parents' house had a secret room in the basement—a cellar where they kept their fine elven wines—and my mother hid me there. When the house was set on fire, the debris fell in front of the cellar door and blocked it. I lay down there, or so I was told, wrapped in one of my mother's traveling cloaks, crying.

The day following the raid, a stranger to the village rode into town alone and searched the rubble. He later told me that when he found me, a single, smoldering chunk of wood lay beside me—a piece of a ceiling beam that had fallen—and it had missed me by mere inches, but had kept me warm. I was alive, awake, staring at him. I even smiled at him, he told me. He smiled back then gently lifted me and carried me away from that ruined place.

We rode hard for a day and a night to the south, into the High Forest. His horse ran tirelessly, swift and surefooted even as night fell and the darkness of the old forest deepened.

The man delivered me into the safety of a small cave, into the arms of a skilled healer. Elbeth, she was called, and she was a caretaker of the forest—a druid. The man delivered me then rode away, and Elbeth never spoke a word of him again.

R.A. & Geno Salvatore

From that day on, Elbeth fed me—mostly the fruits and berries that grew wild throughout the area—and she kept me clothed and sheltered. She taught me to speak, and showed me the ways of the forest animals.

"Lucky child," Elbeth called me. I had no real name, and she had no inclination to give me one. A name did not define a person, she said. Instead, it merely marked things for recognition, like the beasts and the trees, and she needed no help to recognize me.

The anniversary of my arrival in the forest served as my birthday. The sixth of those days dawned dimly, the skies overcast with dense clouds. The rain began about noontime. The skies grew darker and darker as rumbles of summer thunder rolled through the trees.

Lightning pierced the sky as a figure strode to the mouth of our little cave, the brilliant bolts illuminating his silhouette, revealing his elf features. His skin was the golden red of an oak leaf in the early autumn, his hair the black of a raven's wing, long and silky and whipping in the rising wind. He moved with grace, and when he spoke his voice was soft and kind. But his eyes betrayed the lie behind that softness. They were dark, and hard, and empty of life.

"You cannot have him," Elbeth said before the strange elf could speak.

"That is not for you to decide, witch," he replied.

"I did not decide," she said. "He came to my door, and I sheltered him, and he needs my shelter still. So here he will stay. You cannot have him—you may not take him."

The elf's hand moved to his shoulder—toward the hilt of the sword sheathed against his back.

Elbeth laughed. "You wish to fight me, do you? Here, now, in my grove, in my home, you think you can defeat me?" She laughed again, and there was weight in her voice.

A flash and a tremendous burst of thunder shook the cave. I jumped, so startled that I tripped over my own feet and landed hard on my backside.

The elf scowled, again reaching for the hilt of

his sword, and again stopping short. He started to speak then looked down at a spot on the ground less than five feet in front of him, blackened and charred where the lightning bolt had struck. In front of him—inside the cave.

"The next one does not miss," Elbeth said, her voice steady.

Still scowling, the strange elf turned on his heel and strode away from the cave.

As soon as he was gone, the wind whipped into a furious gale and the downpour began.

Elbeth turned to me. "Let's have some supper, shall we? It is your birthday, after all."

"Who was that?" I asked.

I wanted to ask about the lightning as well. Elbeth had told me lightning prefers to hit the tallest object in an area, yet we were in a cave at the base of a hill surrounded by tall trees and the bolt had found its way through. But she seemed not to worry, so I took comfort in her confidence.

"He is none of your concern," she answered. "Just an old acquaintance." She waved her hand,

The Stowaway

spoke a few words, and suddenly the stone slab that served as a table was covered with a feast— sweet, sun-ripened fruits from the forest and a rare treat: heavy, sugared cream.

I dug right in. Elbeth stood at the mouth of the cave for a few moments, singing to the forest rain before she came to join me.

Despite the rain, the air was warm, and as always, the company was pleasant. Elbeth had a warm smile and hearty laugh, and our friends— small woodland creatures—joined us whenever we had a feast. I especially loved the chipmunks and squirrels, little rodents running up the sides of our cave as if gravity did not effect them. One particular chipmunk loved me too—or at least loved the berries and nuts I would save from my meals to share with him. He grabbed a berry off our stone table then ducked into a corner to nibble on it. I laughed at his boldness and tossed him a few more.

As darkness fell, with the rain continuing as hard as ever, the food ran out—though we were all long since full—and the animals cleared out to find their own shelters. I settled into my soft goose down bed to sleep.

When I awoke, I could not tell the hour. It was night and the rain continued, perhaps even more heavily, and the fire inside the cave had been doused. Elbeth crouched by the doorway, looking out into the forest. Something was amiss—I could tell instantly.

The forest was far too bright. Orange light seemed to pour in from every direction, despite the rain and the late hour. I pulled myself from my bed and crawled to the mouth of the cave.

The sight that greeted me was the most frightening thing I had ever seen. Sheets of flame rose up against the downpour. In all directions, the forest was ablaze; howls of the woodland creatures pierced the air. I took Elbeth's hand, but the cold sweat that covered it did little to comfort my fears. I looked at her face and saw, to my surprise, that her eyes were closed.

Not sure what to do, I closed my eyes, too. I focused on the sounds, and after only a moment I heard what Elbeth was listening to: a voice.

The Stowaway

"Come out of your cave, witch," said the voice—the same voice I had heard earlier that day, the voice of that strange elf. "Come out of your cave, and let us see who is the stronger. Or sit and wait and let me burn the whole forest around you."

I opened my eyes and looked at Elbeth. A blue jay landed on her shoulder, chirped out a few notes, then swept back into the drenched forest. Elbeth turned to me, an unfamiliar expression on her face—fear.

"Come, Lucky Child, we must fly from this place." She cast her cloak over me and gripped my hand. Together we raced out into the downpour.

The storm intensified. The lump of fear that had formed in my chest from the moment the stranger had arrived filled my whole body. My arms felt numb with cold but the muscles in my legs burned as Elbeth pushed me to move faster than I had ever run before.

Once in a while, I tugged on her hand. "Please—can we stop for a moment and rest?"

"Not yet," Elbeth said, and she urged me to run faster, deeper into the forest.

R.A. & Geno Salvatore

After what seemed like hours, suddenly and without explanation, she slowed and veered off her course to a pine tree overgrown with vines.

She pointed toward the sheltered boughs. "There, Lucky Child. Now you rest."

I heaved a sigh and flopped down upon the pine needles. I bent over to rub my aching calves.

Above my head, Elbeth moved her hands in a circle, slowly chanting. As she finished, I felt my skin go prickly. It changed color, turning darker and rougher until it matched the hue and texture of the tree's trunk.

"Do not move," she said to me gently. "And do not cry out. Tomorrow, find the road and follow it. Someone will find you. The animals will help."

I swallowed hard and took a deep breath. "But you're coming back, aren't you?" I said, trying not to cry.

"If I can." She smiled. "But you are Lucky Child, remember? Everything will be all right. Everything always works out for the best."

Her smile faded and she turned back to the

forest, toward the fires. I imagined the elf's voice echoing all around us.

As she moved away, I saw her crouch down on all fours. I saw her limbs thicken and lengthen, and her clothing melt into fur.

Soon, not a woman but a great brown bear was striding into the woods, roaring angrily, challenging the strange elf to face her.

As Elbeth raced away, I finally allowed my tears to fall. But only for a moment. Then I did as I had been told: I ducked under the boughs of the pine tree and soon drifted off to sleep.

R.A. & Geno Salvatore

Chapter Eight

"Wake up, child." The man's voice was somehow comforting, though I could not say why. "Wake up, young one. We must be off at once."

I opened my eyes. It was still raining, though it had turned from a downpour to a drizzle. The sky was pitch black except for the flicker of light coming from the sputtering torch in the man's hand.

The man gripped my arm and tried to pull me to my feet. "Come," he repeated, "we must hurry."

I wrenched my arm out of his grip and shook my head. "I am to stay here until dawn, then follow the road if Elbeth isn't back." At the mention of her name, the man winced.

"Elbeth is not coming back, child. You are to come with me now. I will take care of you."

"But where is Elbeth?" In my heart, I already knew the answer. She was in the same place as my first family. I swallowed the lump that rose in my throat.

He winced, and tried to speak several times before he finally managed to utter one syllable, his voice cracking slightly. "Gone."

There was a strange finality to the way he said it. He reached out his hand again. "Come. We must be away before he returns."

For some reason, I was not afraid any longer. The look on the man's face when I had spoken Elbeth's name told me that I could trust him. And the thought of venturing out alone on the road seemed more frightening than following the man who promised to watch over me.

I took his hand. He pulled me to my feet

R.A. & Geno Salvatore

then lifted me into his arms and carried me to his horse. After he helped me climb into the saddle, he slid in gracefully behind me, taking the reins and spurring the animal forward.

"Ever ridden a horse before, child?"

"No, sir." I ran my hand along the beast's mane. It felt surprisingly thick and coarse.

He gently patted her white coat. "This is Haze, as true a friend as you'll find in all Faerûn," he said.

She was beautiful, her coat glistening in the rain yet warm to the touch. I felt something different about her, different from all the animals I had known in the High Forest. She felt—magical, somehow.

"Where are we going, sir?" I asked hesitantly. Elbeth had told me the world was a large place, but had failed to give any details. The world I knew was a small cave in a sheltered grove in the middle of the High Forest. But that place was gone and I was riding into the unknown. I tightened my grip on this stranger's deep blue cloak.

"Wherever the road leads," he said gently. "And

The Stowaway

don't call me sir. Call me Perrault." He smiled.

"So, boy, what name do you go by? What did she call you?" he asked me, rubbing his neatly trimmed gray goatee. He peered at me thoughtfully, his blue eyes flashing. He was trying to ask the question lightly, but there was pain in his voice.

"I haven't a name, mister Perrault. She just called me 'Lucky Child,' 'cause I was lucky to live long enough to meet her."

"Yes. Yes, you were lucky, my boy, but that doesn't mean you shouldn't have a proper name. Twice lucky, now, to be alive to meet me again. Twice lucky . . ." He paused in thought. "There is a name I have heard of in my travels—a word in the language of the nomads of the Great Desert. *Maimun*, they sometimes title their children, and it means 'twice lucky.'" He smiled at me. "Maimun. What do you think, my boy? Does the name fit you?"

I shrugged.

"Well, try it out then!" he said.

"Maimun. Maimun." I spoke softly at first, letting the word roll out of my mouth naturally. As I gained confidence in it, my voice grew

R.A. & Geno Salvatore

louder and a grin broke out on my face. "Yes, mister Perrault, it . . . fits me. Maimun, the twice lucky child." And then I remembered all that had happened, and a lump rose in my throat. "Only I don't feel lucky, mister Perrault. I want to see Elbeth again."

He wrapped his arm more tightly around me and began to hum a slow, sad tune, which soon turned into an even sadder song. He sang in a language I did not understand, but I knew he was singing to Elbeth, saying his farewell. The rain fell gently around us, but the drops never seemed to reach us.

As Haze carried us through the forest, my sadness began to lift. The sun peeked over the horizon, and orange and fuchsia painted the sky.

I looked at Perrault; he looked back at me, and managed a smile. The pain showed through his expression, but it did nothing to diminish the happiness in his bright eyes.

"Look there, to the east," he said. "Smile at the sunrise, for a new day has begun, and that is a beautiful thing."

"Why is it beautiful?" I asked. My tongue was thick from crying and the word fell awkwardly off my lips.

"Every day is a chance to start over. Any day can be bad, surely, but any day can be good, can be great, and that promise, that potential, is a beautiful thing indeed. And today will be a good day, little Maimun," he said. I heard a distinctly upbeat ring in his voice. "Today is the beginning of our new journey. Today we begin our ride to the south and to the east. The wind has come up, and I can feel it in my hair and on my skin. I can taste the salt on the breeze. Can you?"

I stopped and considered this odd question for a moment then shook my head. The air felt perfectly fresh, not at all salty.

He laughed. "You will, my boy, you will. Today we begin the adventure of your life. Tell me, little Maimun, have you ever seen the ocean? Did Elbeth ever take you there?"

Again I shook my head.

"Then you are in for quite a treat."

Chapter Nine

"Did you know there's a dragon living directly beneath our feet?" I asked.

"Well then, we'd best watch where we step," Perrault replied. His head never rose from the book on his lap.

Nearly six years had passed since Perrault had rescued me from beneath the boughs of the pine tree. He had kept his promise of showing me the ocean. From the High Forest we had headed directly to the Sword Coast, and we spent the following years wandering the lands along the sea.

We slept outside or in a tent during the summer months. In the winter, we took shelter in the homes of farmers, who were always willing to share their hospitality for an evening of Perrault's stories.

Perrault loved to travel and after several days in one place, he would grow restless and insist it was time for us to move on. I longed for a real home, but Perrault said people like us weren't meant to be tied down to one place. So all I had to call my own was a bedroll.

That same night, after setting up camp and cooking our supper, Perrault stoked the fire and we both pulled out our books.

"The dragon's name is Adraedan," I explained, after consulting the heavy book on my lap, "and he was imprisoned beneath these hills by the Uthgardt barbarians. He was digging up the sacred burial places of the tribes, so they all got together and chose the best warriors from each tribe. They formed a new tribe, and they called themselves the Tribe of the Dragon." I turned the page and stared at our campfire's glowing embers. "Perrault, do you think my family might have belonged to such a tribe?"

"Read in silence, Maimun." Perrault didn't look up from the tome in front of him. "I have business to attend."

I was not surprised by his gruff answer. For the most part, Perrault was quick to answer most of my questions. He had taught me much about the world, from the names of the cities and small towns lining the Sword Coast to the great tales of the history of Faerûn. When the nightmares of Elbeth and the blazing forest woke me in a cold sweat, he would sit up late into the night, pointing out constellations and counting the stars with me until I fell asleep.

But when I asked him to tell me about the night of the fire or anything related to my past, he never gave me the answers I desired, save for the barest of details. I had learned that the night of the High Forest fire—the night of my sixth birthday— was not the first time Perrault had come to my aid. Perrault told me the tale of my rescue from my parents' home, and how he had delivered me into Elbeth's care. But any more than that, he did not know or would not say.

I sighed—loudly, but Perrault did not notice—and went back to reading the tale of the great battle between the Tribe of the Dragon and the mighty wyrm Adraedan, fought not a mile from the very ground I lay upon.

Like me, Perrault had a tome lying open before him. It was the only book among his extensive collection I was not permitted to read: a great, black, leather-bound thing with a heavy brass lock. I had never seen the key Perrault used to open the book—even though I'd hunted for it, had searched every place I could think of.

I only wanted to peek inside, to know what the book contained. It had no title, and I was desperate to know what secrets it might hold between its plain black covers. But the point was moot—I had never found the key.

Our campfire burned lower and my eyes grew heavy. I closed my book and carried it to the sack that contained Perrault's modest library. From the outside, the bag appeared to be a normal haversack,

R.A. & Geno Salvatore

a satchel with a strap to sling over the shoulder. But the bag was enchanted to hold far more than should have been possible. I was pretty sure I could have fit inside that sack along with all the books.

I quickly scanned through the meticulously organized stacks of books, finding the appropriate place for the one I had been reading—in between *Demons and Devils* and *The Elven Folk.*

The bag held hundreds more books of all shapes and sizes. With those books, Perrault had taught me to read. And after six years on the road with Perrault, I had read each book in the collection at least once. Each book, that is, save one— that unmarked black tome.

With another sigh, I closed the sack and turned toward my bedroll. The night was warm, and the day's journey had been a long and hard ride across the rolling hills of the Crags, so I would surely sleep well.

I began to climb into bed, to wrap myself in a light blanket and in dreams of the mighty dragon I had been reading about. But Perrault's voice stopped me.

The Stowaway

"Hold it. Back to the bag." I looked up to see him holding the black tome—closed and locked, I noted. I cursed myself silently. I had, for the thousandth time, missed the opportunity to catch a glimpse of the key.

I could not quite decipher the look Perrault leveled at me.

"It's all organized and neat, sir," I said hesitantly. "I put my book back right where it belongs."

"I do not doubt that. But I need you to fetch another book." The request was highly unusual—Perrault knew every book in the bag by heart, so the requested book could not be for him to read. But he rarely tried to guide my reading, instead allowing me to explore the books at my own pace.

"Which one?" I asked.

"*The Travels of Volo*. There should be a volume describing the central Sword Coast."

I reached into the bag, quickly pulling forth the appropriate book.

I was intrigued. In our six years of wandering,

R.A. & Geno Salvatore

we had visited the northern Sword Coast and the southern Sword Coast, but we had always avoided everything between Waterdeep and Tyr. Perrault had never told me the reason, and I had never asked.

Perhaps that was about to change.

"Inside should be a description of the city of Baldur's Gate."

I nodded, and flipped open the book to that section and began reading. "'A thriving trade port and crossroads, Baldur's Gate lies halfway between Waterdeep and Calimport, and serves as a layover point for travel and trade in both directions, as well as . . .'"

Perrault's upraised hand stopped me. "Tomorrow, instead of dragons and barbarians and ancient battles, you will read that passage, until you know every word."

"Are we going there? Are we going to Baldur's Gate?" I asked, trying to keep the obvious hope out of my voice. I had never been inside a real city before—nothing larger than the town of Nesmé on the Evermoors. From afar, I had glimpsed mighty Waterdeep. The massive sprawl, the great mansions . . . the idea of tens of thousands of people living so close together was foreign to me. And in my mind, anything foreign, anything unknown, was worth investigating.

"As always, we are going where the road takes us," Perrault replied. "Where that will next be, I cannot say. But it is best to be prepared. Now, time for bed. Get some rest. We have a long day's ride ahead of us, and another after that."

Perrault turned away from me before I could respond, the surest sign he could offer that the conversation was finished. With a shrug, I put the book in the bag. I did not place the rich tome, penned by the incomparable traveler Volo, among the many other works in Perrault's collection. Instead, I placed it on top of the stack, in ready reach for the next day.

I went to my sleeping mat, lay down, and soon I was asleep. I dreamed of Baldur's Gate. I hadn't finished reading the passage about the city yet, but that did not stop my wandering mind from inventing all the necessary details.

R.A. & Geno Salvatore

I found little time to read the book the next day. We were up at dawn, as usual. It's difficult to remain asleep outdoors once the sun comes up. We rode for the entire day, stopping only for a brief lunch. We didn't ride too hard, but the landscape was uneven, and riding over such terrain is tiring. By the time we'd set our night's camp under a cloudless and moonlit sky, I had hardly the energy to lift the book, let alone read it.

The next day was the same, and the third and the fourth and the fifth. Each morning, when I awoke, Perrault would ask me how much I had read the day past. And each morning, I would answer that I had not read at all. Perrault would give me a slight nod, a sarcastic expression that told me he was trying to teach me something, though I hadn't the slightest idea what.

On the sixth day, the terrain changed. We quit the hills and turned southeast. We followed no road, but the land was flat and the run was easy. Farms dotted the landscape, their crops grown large in the summer heat. And what heat there was on that journey—not a cloud in the sky for the next twelve days, the sun bright and beautiful and scorching.

Despite the heat, our pace increased. I sensed a furor in Perrault, a desire to be at our destination as soon as possible. I shared the same desire, though I was sure our reasons were different. I wanted to see Baldur's Gate—I assumed that was our destination, though Perrault denied he had a location in mind. I thrilled at the thought of stepping inside a real city for the first time in my life. Perrault seemed only anxious, nervous, like he was on a dangerous mission and wanted the task completed.

The journey was not like any other we had taken. We had often traveled in uncivilized lands, where farms stood alone and held only nominal ties to a village. But even in the summer, even when we needed no shelter, we would stop at farmhouses along the way to exchange news and stories, and perhaps take a meal.

This time, we didn't pause at a single home

or inn, didn't stop anywhere except to set camp. Our line was as straight as Perrault could manage, and we rode as fast as Haze could carry us without tiring.

My twelfth birthday passed without any mention from Perrault. He had never been one for grand celebrations, though he would normally give me some token to mark that one more year had passed since he discovered me in the ashes of my parents' home. But I didn't complain. I hoped my birthday gift lay at the end of our hard journey.

Around midday of the seventeenth day after Perrault charged me with reading Volo's description of Baldur's Gate, we crested a low, rocky ridge and saw spread out before us the mighty city. The sight took my breath away.

Perhaps four miles off, down a long green slope, it was more massive than I ever imagined. A great sprawl spread east and west, ending at a massive wall that I imagined was a hundred feet tall. Toward the center I could see another wall, surrounding a steep hill covered with massive

93

structures, beautiful and graceful temples, great white towers ascending skyward like arrows aimed at the sun. The city rested on the banks of the mighty River Chionthar, which cut through the land to the sea like a great blue snake, wider than the city, twisting and turning its way through the green plain from the low hills to the east—toward the hills we stood upon.

"How many people live there?" I asked breathlessly.

"If you had read the passage, you would know the answer to that." Perrault motioned for me to dismount and I slipped off Haze's back as gracefully as I could.

I winced. "We rode too hard and I was too tired. I'm sorry, sir."

"So you did not learn the lesson I assigned you. But you learned a more important one in the process, did you not?"

"I don't know. Did I?"

"What do you expect you would have found, had you read the passage?" Perrault asked. I heard no anger in his voice.

"I don't know. Probably, the population and size and who runs it and who the important people are and things like that."

"Indeed." Perrault swung his leg over Haze's back and jumped to the ground. "And you would have found an accurate description of the docks, plus a list of fine inns worth staying at, monuments worth seeing, and the best market to buy your goods from. Here we are about to enter the city, and you know none of that because you did not read the passage."

"It wasn't fair! We were traveling all day and into the night. I didn't have time—"

"Life is not defined by how much time you have." Perrault was looking right at me, and I was surprised to see that there was no disappointment on his face. "It is about time you have *to spare.* You had seventeen days to read one simple passage—in the two days prior, you probably read more than that. And yet you chose not to spare the time. It is the smallest of choices that shape our destinies."

He turned away and gazed out down the

The Stowaway

hill toward Baldur's Gate. "Now, we must make our meal and rest a while. We enter the city at sunset."

R.A. & Geno Salvatore

Chapter Ten

I could hardly wait for sunset. I spent most of the dying hours of daylight moving about our small campsite, alternately staring at the looming specter of Baldur's Gate, or trying my best to put the city out of my mind. I groomed Haze, though she needed no grooming. I delved into Volo's account of Baldur's Gate, but it only heightened my anticipation. I tried closing my eyes and taking a nap. But none of it worked, and the harder I tried to put aside my excitement for the night's adventure, the more fully it occupied my thoughts.

After an eternity, the sun touched the western horizon, and we gathered our packs and headed for the city.

We carried no light—the risk of being seen was far too great. Though he never told me why, Perrault was determined to enter the city in secret. The walk across those four miles seemed unbearably long. With the city and its secrets just out of my reach, the anticipation as that distance became smaller and smaller was too much to take. But then, before I could blink, we were pressed up against the city's outer parapet.

I glanced up at the wall. I could see a torch directly above us, where at least one guard patrolled, but he was roaming toward the much larger flame anchoring the northeastern corner of the wall. A few other guards with torches moved along the wall, but none drifted near our position.

I looked to Perrault and saw him setting a coil of rope on the ground. As I watched, he began to hum a low tune, and he swayed gently back and forth. The rope rose up as a snake might, swaying

R.A. & Geno Salvatore

in time with him. Slowly, so slowly, it ascended into the air, completely unsupported, until the end of the rope reached the top of the wall.

Perrault stopped humming and the rope stopped swaying. Perrault took hold and gave the rope a tug, smiling when it didn't fall down on us.

"Come on then, up we go," he said.

Without looking at me, he began to scale the wall. I followed a few moments later. As I reached the parapet, Perrault held out a hand through the crenellations and hauled me onto the wall. My hands felt raw and my arms burned, but Perrault had not even broken a sweat. For an older man, he was surprisingly strong.

After a quick glance to confirm that no one was around, Perrault reached out, grabbed the rope, and whispered a single word beneath his breath. The rope jumped up, twisting into a perfect coil in his hand. He slipped the rope into his pack, and pulled out two gold rings.

"Now comes the fun part," he whispered.

I could see the mischievous twinkle in his eye,

despite the darkness. He slipped one of the rings onto a finger, and handed me the other. I followed suit and slipped the much-too-large ring onto the middle finger of my right hand. As soon as I let go of it, the band shrank to fit my finger perfectly.

"All right," Perrault whispered, "I'll count to three, and when I say three, we jump." He motioned to the inside of the wall, which was not crenellated. I stole a glance over the edge—it was more than twenty feet, and unlike the grassy field on the outside, the inside was a street of cobbled stones. I looked up at Perrault, and I could see him holding back a chuckle.

"Trust me," he said, and he took my hand.

He put his toes against the edge of the wall. With a deep, steadying gulp, I followed suit. I tried not to look down, but of course that was impossible, and the view turned my stomach and made me dizzy.

"One," he said, low and under his breath.

I thought I noted a trace of fear in his speech, but with the supreme voice control Perrault had

R.A. & Geno Salvatore

developed from singing for so long, he could have hidden that undertone there just to unnerve me. He would get some amusement from that.

"Two," he said, a little louder.

The note of fear was clearer, but as I heard the clack-clacking of hooves approaching on the cobblestones, I realized his fear was no joke. I thought I should suggest we wait until whoever was approaching had passed, but before I could say anything I saw torchlight coming down the wall from the west. The darkness offered some concealment, but it seemed unlikely that the guard with the torch would miss us. We would have to jump, and hope the man approaching—

"Three!"

I felt a tug at my hand as Perrault leaped from the wall, and I jumped with him. A scream built inside me as my feet left solid ground, but I swallowed it.

As soon as we left the wall, I felt the ring on my finger grow slightly warm. I was not falling, but was drifting downward like a feather in a gentle breeze. I looked to Perrault, who had released my hand, to see him gently descending too. As he "fell," he reached into his pack and pulled out another object, too small for me to see.

The clack-clack of hooves grew louder, and before we landed I saw a man dressed in the uniform of the Baldur's Gate city guard trot around the corner. He was mounted atop a tall brown horse and held a torch in one hand, his spear resting casually across the front of the saddle.

"Oy, you there, speak and be recognized!" he said as we landed, his voice trembling slightly.

"Oh, sir, I would, but as it were, I prefer to remain anonymous," Perrault said. "So sorry."

He tossed the item he was holding in the direction of the guard. I saw it glint as it arced through the torchlight—it looked like a glass bead. Before I could get a clear view of it, it struck the ground at the foot of the guardsman's horse with a slight *pop*. As it broke, wisps of energy flowed up and around the guard, quickly weaving themselves into a solid, translucent bubble.

The guard recoiled and nearly fell off his horse. "Oy, what trickery is this?"

I could barely hear him. His voice was muffled by the magical bubble. He grabbed his spear and thrust it at the bubble, but it merely bounced off. He slid off his horse and tried to push through the sphere, but it proved unyielding.

I glanced up at the wall and saw the flicker of a guard's torch moving along the battlement.

The trapped guard saw his comrade on top of the wall. He stabbed wildly with his spear at the top of the bubble, to no effect, and screamed at the top of his lungs, though barely any sound passed through the magical barrier.

The man on the wall didn't hear him, and the torchlight moved on.

The guard's horse whinnied angrily at its master's yelling and put its head on the guard's shoulder, using its weight to push him to the ground.

The guard struggled, shoving the horse's head aside and trying—unsuccessfully—to stand, all the while yelling. That only annoyed the beast more. As the guard cursed and spat, the horse laid down, trapping the guardsman's legs beneath its belly.

The Stowaway

The watchman finally stopped yelling.

"Sorry, sir, but as I say, I prefer anonymity. This orb will guarantee that. Anyway, the bubble will fade. Eventually." Perrault's smile could easily have belonged to a troublemaking child, yet it somehow fit just as perfectly on his weathered face.

He turned to me and said, "Come, boy, we have appointments to keep."

R.A. & Geno Salvatore

Chapter Eleven

Baldur's Gate was unlike anything I had ever seen. Traveling through the city that night, hardly a person was to be found—the only people on the streets were the vagabonds who had nowhere else to go, the guards on patrol, and those rogues who had managed to avoid the notice of the guards.

We fell into the rogue category, slipping through the cobblestone streets by moonlight. Occasionally I glanced up at the stars to determine the direction we traveled. But with all the buildings crowding around us, it was difficult to keep any significant portion of the sky in sight, and the city's roads were twisting and narrow.

We wound our way among old, run-down buildings and newer structures. At first, I tried to identify places from the map of the city in Volo's account, but we moved too fast and soon I gave up.

The sights were not impressive, but I found the smell of the place quite pleasant. The salt air of the ocean hung thickly over the city, where it combined with various spices and incenses brought for trade from all across Faerûn. The steady breeze mixed the aromas together into a soothing fragrance.

We roamed for a time, often ducking into alleys to avoid a passing guard.

At last Perrault stepped up to a closed doorway beneath a faded old sign displaying a drained mug and the establishment's name, The Empty Flagon. No light shone in the windows or door, and no sound pierced the night.

I figured the place was deserted. As Perrault opened the door, I saw I was correct. The tavern was empty. Stools were set on tables, and no one stood behind the bar.

"Well, what are you waiting for?" Perrault asked. "Head on in!" Again, that twinkle in his eye signaled mischief to me.

I hesitated for a moment, but Perrault just stood there. He would never do anything that would cause me real harm, I knew, so it was time to see what the game was.

I felt something strange as I stepped into the room, a sort of uneasiness, but I could not figure out what it was. I walked, slowly and cautiously, to the bar, looking around but seeing nothing. The tavern had no other exits save the way I had entered. I turned back to the door, seeing Perrault standing outside.

"There's nothing here," I called to him. "The place is empty."

"How would you know that?" he asked. His voice was quiet, yet I heard him quite clearly. "You haven't even entered the room."

"What do you mean?" I asked. "I'm inside . . ." I turned, sweeping my hand out wide. But as I

The Stowaway

turned to where the bar had been, I realized I was staring into the room—from the outside, as if I were still at the threshold.

"Behold the power of illusion," he said with a laugh. "Now, let's head in." He spoke a few words—"Good ale and fine stories,"—stepped across the threshold, and vanished.

I blinked a few times and looked around, but I could not see my mentor anywhere. I saw only one option.

"Good ale and fine stories," I mumbled, and in I stepped.

I crossed the threshold into sudden blinding light and a chorus of voices talking, shouting, singing, and cheering. As my eyes adjusted and I looked around, I saw an entirely different room. Every table was occupied, every chair filled—except a few whose occupants had fallen out in a drunken stupor—and many more people were standing or were seated on the floor around the hearth. Many of the patrons were not human, I noticed, and especially prominent were the dwarves and gnomes. Half a dozen women moved

R.A. & Geno Salvatore

around the room, carrying trays that patrons simply plucked drinks from as they moved past.

Around the fire was gathered a group of dwarves, standing arm in arm and mug in hand, singing loud, raucous drinking songs—which, to dwarves, apparently meant songs about killing goblins. At each reference to a new and creative means of killing goblins, whether smashing goblin heads with rocks, bashing goblin skulls with hammers, or crushing goblin noggins with . . . another goblin, the dwarves let out a loud cheer.

They sang in detail exactly how to use a goblin as a weapon—hold him by the ankles, spin in place to build momentum, then slam him down in an overhead chop as if swinging a battle-axe. I knew from my reading that the goblin's head is the hardest part, and the best results are reached when the goblins hit head to head. The sound of the cracking can be quite loud and clear, and pleasing to the ear.

In all my years of traveling with Perrault, I had never seen anything like the place. And I couldn't help but listen, imagining the stocky,

The Stowaway

sturdy people swinging ugly goblins by the ankles, using the nasty creatures as weapons against themselves. Probably a sport in dwarven cities, I mused. I decided that someday I would have to travel to dwarf lands and see it firsthand.

"Perrault, my friend, it is good to see you again." A voice to my side, distinct among the crowd, broke the trance the dwarves' singing had induced.

I turned to see Perrault moving easily toward the bar through the crush of dwarves.

From the sound of the voice, I had expected a human or perhaps an elf, but I was surprised to see an old, gray-bearded dwarf balanced on a small pulsing blue disk of energy, drifting up and over the bar. Perrault and the dwarf talked, but their voices were low and I could not make out what they were saying.

I crept closer.

". . . waiting for you upstairs, but a man from her temple came calling and she left in a hurry. She said to leave it for—" The dwarf broke off his sentence abruptly and turned to look at me.

R.A. & Geno Salvatore

Under that piercing gaze, I suddenly felt naked, and I felt ashamed. I had sneaked into the conversation uninvited. I tried to sink into the crowd, but the dwarf's eyes softened and his thick lips turned up in a smile. His brilliant white teeth showed brightly through his dense beard.

"And this must be your ward, then," he said. Though the statement was obviously directed at Perrault, the dwarf's eyes never left me.

Perrault turned to look at me. There was surprise and, I thought, a bit of approval in that look. I knew immediately that Perrault had not noticed me, and was impressed that I had managed to get so close without alerting his attention.

"Yes, yes. This is my boy, my young apprentice," Perrault said, quickly composing himself. "Maimun, this is Alviss. He's a dear old friend. A bit surly—" he cast the dwarf a sidelong glance, to which Alviss only rolled his eyes and widened his grin— "but he's offered to watch you for me tonight."

"Watch me?" I asked. "I don't need anyone to watch me. Where are you going, and why can't I come?"

"I have business to attend, and it is not your concern. You stay here with Alviss. He'll give you a bed, and you can get some sleep." Perrault looked at Alviss as he spoke, and the dwarf was nodding before he finished.

"I'll give you a cot in the common room. It's mostly empty, anyway."

The dwarf put his hand on my shoulder and started to lead me away, but Perrault stopped him with an upraised hand. He leaned in close to Alviss and said under his breath, "Keep your eyes open. I'll be coming back fast and I'll need the boy ready to run."

Alviss nodded. Before I could say anything, he was leading me away to the common room and Perrault was exiting the tavern the same way we'd come in.

R.A. & Geno Salvatore

Chapter Twelve

I couldn't sleep that night either.

I forced my eyes shut, tried to empty all thought from my mind, tried to embrace the weariness in my body, but despite my best efforts, my thoughts kept racing back to Perrault and his secret appointment.

After what seemed an eternity, I gave up, pulled myself from my cot, and dressed. I snuck to the door of the common room, quiet as a ghost so as not to disturb the two other people who had taken cots there, and put my ear against the portal. I heard nothing beyond.

Slowly, gently, I pushed the door open.

The tavern was empty of patrons, the chairs all placed atop the tables, the freshly mopped floor glistening. The only light in the room came from the bar—the pulsing blue glow of Alviss's magical floating disc. And there sat the old dwarf, mindlessly wiping down the bar with a rag and humming to himself.

Alviss seemed sufficiently preoccupied, and the room sufficiently shadowy, for me to cross the room without being seen. The exit was almost directly opposite the doorway in which I stood, so I would have to cross a lot of open space.

I moved quickly, keeping my weight on my toes—I had read a passage in one of Perrault's books detailing the proper way to move stealthily—and I used the tables for cover. The floor was slick, but not excessively, and soon I was reaching for the handle of the front door.

Alviss was still humming tunelessly and running the cloth over the bar. As soon as I touched the door, though, the old graybeard jumped.

He turned to look right at me.

He clapped his hands twice, the sharp noise shattering the silence, and the room was suddenly as bright as it had been that evening when Perrault and I had arrived.

Alviss stared at me. I thought I saw his lips turn up in a bit of a smile, but it could have been the wrinkles on his weathered face. "Now, now, young'n, there's no way I'll be letting you wander out into the streets alone!" he said. "It isn't safe, you know."

"I won't get in any trouble. I don't get caught. You wouldn't have noticed me except for that . . . magic." I would have continued my protest except I saw Alviss, barely holding in a chuckle, patting his hands in the air to calm me down.

"I did not mean it wasn't safe for *you,*" he said, a laugh escaping his lips. "I mean, it wouldn't be safe for *me* should Perrault return to find out I had let his nosey young ward out alone to follow him to a private appointment!" The dwarf's chuckle turned into a great belly laugh. On and on it went, sounding so out of place coming from that soft-spoken creature. After a moment I joined in.

He stopped laughing abruptly, leaving a note of my high-pitched giggle hanging awkwardly in the air. His face, however, did not lose its mirth—indeed, his smile seemed to widen, his lips curling in an almost sinister fashion.

"Come to think of it, though, all Perrault said to me was, 'keep the boy here.' He said nothing of keeping you from watching him."

"But how can I watch him if I can't leave?"

"Oh, there are ways." He turned and hopped off the magical floating disk—which instantly disappeared—and walked toward a small door hidden behind the bar. As he reached the door, he motioned for me to follow.

"Come, young'n, if you want to see." His voice was barely above a whisper.

I hesitated for only a moment, my curiosity outweighing my apprehension.

I followed Alviss through the tiny door into a pitch-black room beyond. No sooner had I stepped across the threshold than my foot caught on some

R.A. & Geno Salvatore

heavy object on the floor. Down I went, directly into a bookshelf, and down it went in turn.

"Wha . . . what did you . . . watch where you . . . are you *blind?*" Alviss shouted. "Oh, right. Light." He clapped his hands twice, and the room was filled instantly with light as bright as the morning sun. "A dwarf needs no light to see. I still forget humans are not so blessed."

I sat up and looked around, rubbing the stubbed toe on my right foot, and could finally see that I had tripped over a huge tome bound in black leather and unlabelled, almost exactly like Perrault's mysterious book. It rested on a toppled bookshelf, which was precariously perched on top of what looked like a human skull—except it was several times as large, and instead of bone-white it was a fiery red. The contents of the shelf had spilled onto the floor, but many more books and scrolls lay about haphazardly than could have fit on the shelf.

"Well, get up already!" Alviss huffed impatiently. I stood up in one of the few open spaces on the floor and caught my balance.

The Stowaway

Alviss, meanwhile, waved his hands and uttered some arcane words. The toppled furniture tilted upright again, spilling what little of its contents had not yet fallen out. The dwarf waved his hand a second time and many books and scrolls leaped from the floor onto the shelves, piling into whatever space they could fill.

Alviss cleared the room's only table. At its center rested a small object covered by a black cloth.

As soon as I stepped up to the table, Alviss stood straighter, pushing back his broad shoulders. With a flourish, he pulled off the cloth, revealing a clear ball of crystal set atop a pitch-black wrought iron stand.

The dwarf moved a finger to his lips, signaling that I should stay quiet, then began moving his hands slowly in circles above the ball. It took me several moments to realize he had also begun chanting—his voice was so low it was almost inaudible.

Suddenly, all light left the room except a brilliant pale blue hue emanating from the crystal ball. The dwarf's deep chanting changed, the words suddenly ringing with perfect clarity.

I leaned in toward the ball, closer, ever closer, the light growing brighter, the rumbling of Alviss's chant growing louder, louder, deafeningly loud, the blue light washing over me.

Chapter Thirteen

The room was vast, so tall it seemed that clouds should have been circling the tops of the enormous pillars. The floor, the walls, those dozens of great pillars made of pink marble, seamless and flat and shining. Great windows lined the walls, beautiful images appearing in the multicolored glass panes, allowing a dim, eerie light to shine through.

At one end of the massive hall lay an enormous dais, a raised platform three steps above the floor. On the dais knelt a figure, a human perhaps, though in the massive room, it was difficult to judge its size. A simple white robe completely covered the form.

My attention swung to the huge oak door at the other end of the hall. The door parted in the middle, one of its massive halves swinging open only a sliver. Then a man slipped through, seeming small indeed. I instantly recognized the midnight blue cloak slung around his shoulders.

Perrault.

The enormous door silently swung shut behind him as Perrault began the long walk across the room.

The figure on the dais rose and turned to face him. A hand reached up, gracefully pulling the hood back to reveal the most beautiful woman I had ever seen. Raven black hair was tucked behind a pointed ear that matched perfectly her angular face.

She descended the three short steps just as Perrault reached her. It appeared at first as though he would sweep her up in a great hug, but he slowed as he approached, instead grasping her shoulders and smiling gently. She returned the smile and spoke, her musical voice seeming to echo forever, yet somehow not disturbing the stillness that pervaded the great hall.

"My friend, it is so good to see you again. You should—you must!—come more often."

"You know why I do not," the man replied. His voice did not echo at all. It seemed out of place, as if it were not worthy to exist.

"Yes, of course, I know your excuses," she said. "Yet here you are, and there is no indication he has even realized."

"There will never be any indication, until I am accosted."

"You have been accosted before, and you have always escaped."

"But I am no longer concerned for myself. Elbeth's ward travels with me, and he is far more important." As he uttered Elbeth's name, the woman's smile disappeared.

She shook her head. "He is not Elbeth's ward any longer. He is yours, to keep and to keep safe. Even if it means poor Jaide cannot see you." She

The Stowaway

smiled. "Even if my only visitor is the dwarf!"

"At least the dwarf can keep his magical eyes on me," Perrault replied, "so you can hear of my exciting exploits. Perhaps those stories will convince you to reconsider your path, to return you to the road."

Again she shook her head. "My calling is here, for as long as it must be. Though I do believe the road will call to me again, perhaps even to your side. Perhaps I will again see the open air of the wide world, but until then I will stay here, in a world somewhat smaller, though no less beautiful.

"Anyway, to business." She waved a hand around her head, as if to brush off the distractions of the previous conversation. "I know why you have come."

Perrault stepped forward. "The boy turned twelve, and has shown remarkable maturity. He is ready to have it returned to him."

She nodded solemnly, her smile gone, and reached into a pocket in her robe. From inside she withdrew a small object, fist-sized, wrapped in white cloth. She looked at it, then looked at

Perrault, then nodded again, holding out the object for him. "As I said, he is your ward now, so the decision is yours. But as you must care for him, you must care for this. It must not be lost, or he will be lost with it."

He reached out, taking the object reverently, and began to speak. Before any words left his mouth, Jaide rushed forward, wrapping him in a tight hug, her mouth pressed to his ear.

"It must not be lost again," she whispered, then pushed away from him. She turned and walked up the steps, taking her kneeling position. She pulled up her hood and bowed her head.

Perrault seemed as if he wanted to speak, but instead he nodded, turned, and began again the long walk across the enormous hall.

I opened my eyes—or perhaps they had never been shut—and staggered back from the table. I felt as though I had come running directly out of the crystal ball. My ankle caught on another giant book and I bumped into the bookshelf behind me and tumbled to the floor. The parchments on the shelf flew off and buried me in a great avalanche of paper.

From beneath the pile of stale-smelling parchment, I could faintly hear Alviss's chanting. I felt myself caught in the spell and pulled upward, but the tug was not enough to lift me.

I found my bearings and looked up to see Alviss staring at me. "Did that answer your questions, young one?"

"Yes sir. I mean, no sir, it . . . Who is she? Where was that? What . . . ?"

Alviss shook his head vigorously, first side to side then up and down. "Precisely. You sought answers to questions, but the answers were not for you. So you spied, you looked where your eyes did not belong. And what, young one, did you find?"

I pondered this for a while. "More questions. I found no answers and only more questions."

"Precisely. And on that note, it is past time you went to bed," Alviss said. "I hope you will

R.A. & Geno Salvatore

remember this lesson, but I would appreciate it if you don't tell Perrault. He still may kill me if he finds out I helped you spy on him." He began to hum softly as he swept me out of the room, through the tavern, and to my cot.

I did not expect to sleep that night. I kept my eyes shut, but on the backs of my eyelids I saw the image of that woman, that elf, her black hair and her piercing eyes, and her voice, echoing softly, gently, perfectly . . .

"It must not be lost again."

The Stowaway

Chapter Fourteen

"Wake up, child." Perrault stood over my cot, gently nudging my shoulder. He looked as if he'd just come from the road, covered in dirt and sweat. He held my clothes, ready for me to put on. I rose and pulled on my pants, then reached for my shirt.

"Hold on," Perrault said. "Put this on first." He handed me a leather belt studded with silver rivets the size of beans. In the middle of the strap, instead of a buckle, was a small pouch.

I moved to put the belt around my waist, but

Perrault shook his head. "Wear it across your chest, right to left, like a sash. Put the pouch over your heart."

Isn't a sash worn *over* a shirt, and wouldn't it be a finer material than this coarse leather? I thought. But I did as I was asked, or tried to. The leather bit into my back and I couldn't find a comfortable position for it no matter what I tried. After a moment of fumbling, Perrault lent a hand, pulling the strap tight.

With the sash in a relatively comfortable position, I looked at Perrault and my heart nearly stopped. In his hand he held an object, fist-sized and wrapped in white cloth, the object Jaide had handed him earlier that night.

"Wha . . . what is that, sir?" I asked, all traces of weariness gone from my mind. I tried to keep my voice steady, but I was unable. I hoped the crack in my voice wouldn't alert Perrault that I had been spying. I was afraid, if he knew, he might not give the thing to me.

"This," he said with reverence in his voice, "is an heirloom—a gift for you. It has been yours

R.A. & Geno Salvatore

since birth, but it has been hidden here within the city for safekeeping until you were old enough to have it—until today." He extended his hands toward me. He reminded me of a priest holding out a bowl of holy water to his disciple.

Slowly, I reached out and took the object. It was at once heavy and light. It didn't weigh much, but I felt as if I were holding something massive and important in my hand. I unwrapped the white cloth to reveal a black stone, perfectly smooth and perfectly round. As I turned the stone in my hands, it swirled with color—blues and reds, and a line of deep violet all wrapped around one another. It took me a long time to pull my eyes from it and look back at Perrault, who stared at me with a patient expression on his face, as though he'd expected that reaction from me.

"It fits perfectly in the pouch on the sash," he said to me. "Keep it there, and never let it be far from your sight."

"But why?" I stared at the stone in my hand. "What does it do?"

"There will be time later for your questions."

The Stowaway

He handed me my shirt. "Now, we must leave."

"Leave?" I asked. "Leave the inn?"

"Not just the inn. We must leave the city, tonight, and be far away by the time the sun sets."

In the predawn hours, very few people were on the street, and none took any notice of our passage. We walked quickly, for Perrault said running would have attracted the guards' interest. I believe we headed south, but the streets wound and meandered and I had trouble keeping my bearings. Perrault seemed to know exactly where he was going, so I just held on tightly to his blue traveling cloak and followed his lead.

All the while, I held one hand wrapped around the stone, which had settled in perfectly to the hollow in the center of my chest, directly over my heart. I felt a warmth from the stone, like it belonged there, had always belonged there, like I had not been a complete person

R.A. & Geno Salvatore

until that night, when this part of myself had been rejoined to me.

I didn't notice that Perrault had stopped until I walked right into him.

I stepped around Perrault to see the reason for our delay. Standing before us, blocking the road, was a single figure. He looked like an elf, with a slight build and pointed ears. His head was clean shaven and his skin was almost the golden tan of a sun elf, with a hint of red to it.

"You should take more care in your travels," said the elf. He was dressed regally, in fine silks of violet and black, and he leaned heavily on an ornately carved staff of black wood, or perhaps obsidian. "You are far too conspicuous for one holding such sought-after goods." The elf's voice was lower than I expected, a solid baritone completely lacking the musical qualities common to the woodland folk.

"I was wondering when you would show one of your ugly faces, Asbeel," Perrault replied, venom dripping from every word.

"Now, now. Let's not insult one another,"

The Stowaway

he chided. "Instead, let's discuss you turning over what is mine, and me not killing you for it." Asbeel displayed a disarming smile, but it was too wide, and appeared more than a little unsettling.

"It is not yours, and it never has been, wretch," Perrault said.

The smile disappeared from Asbeel's face. "What did I just say about insults, fool?" he asked.

Perrault ignored him, turning instead to me. "Maimun, are you tired?"

I hesitated. "No, I slept plenty."

"Good. Are your shoes tied?"

"Yes sir."

"Excellent. Run."

Immediately I was off and sprinting down the street.

Behind me, I heard a loud *pop,* followed by a sound like the hiss of an oil-soaked rag that had been set afire. I turned to look, but saw only Perrault filling my vision as he ran behind me. He caught me in mid stride and carried me, his strong legs far outpacing any speed I could have

R.A. & Geno Salvatore

managed—far outpacing any speed a human should have been capable of. Behind me, I heard a laugh, deep and menacing, but it quickly faded into the distance.

Perrault ran, turning down every side street we passed. At first, I thought he was lost, but the expression on his face, stern and determined, led me to believe he had a destination in mind. He chanted under his breath as we moved, and once brought a tiny silver whistle to his lips. I had not seen the device before, but I was hardly surprised when the thing made no noise whatsoever as he blew into it. Another unexplained bit of magic, one of a hundred I had seen Perrault use.

We rounded a corner and reached the most open area of the city—the docks. A massive expanse along the banks of the Chionthar, the docks of Baldur's Gate contained no fewer than a hundred wharves, ready to take as many ships as the great ports both north and south could send their way. A road ran along the docks, as wide as four streets in the city, to accommodate the massive rushes of people and cargo getting on or off the ships

The Stowaway

in port. The far side of the road was lined with warehouses, tall and imposing and packed tightly together, giving the impression of a great wall separating the riverfront from the rest of the city.

At that hour, the docks were mostly empty. Only a dozen ships were moored, all at the long wharves on the northern end of the riverfront. Dawn was just about to break—the sky over the hills to the east were lightening to a pale blue to herald the sun's approach. The only bustle was around the ships, as crews rose from their sleep and went about their business. Not a soul wandered anywhere around us.

No one, save the pair of burning red eyes emerging from the shadows of the warehouse beside us.

Chapter Fifteen

Asbeel stepped out, grinning a horrible grin. He looked taller than before, his skin redder and not so perfectly smooth. He circled behind us, cutting off our route back to the alley we had just exited, but leaving open the wide street along the docks.

Perrault turned and ran down the street with all haste.

But Asbeel was in front of us, laughing.

The elf—or the creature that appeared as an elf—lunged forward. Perrault dropped me and leaped to meet him, producing from his boot a slender dagger. He sliced the stiletto through the air a few times to keep the creature at bay. I backed up, scrambling to put distance between myself and Asbeel, but not wanting to take my eyes off the spectacle.

Perrault advanced, advanced, advanced, swinging all the while. Asbeel gave ground, using his staff for defense, laughing all the while.

Then Asbeel was gone.

I felt a hand grip my shoulder—iron-strong claws digging into my flesh.

Perrault realized immediately what had happened. He turned and sprinted at me, but he was too late. I felt myself lifted off the ground.

I turned my head to see the creature holding me, no longer an elf but some demonic thing, half again the height of a man, covered in red scales, with great red wings extending from his shoulders. On his face was that same unsettling grin.

His wings beat once, then again, and up we rose a few feet, then a few more. I tried to grab his hand, to wrench it free of me, but his grip was too strong and I had no way to break it.

R.A. & Geno Salvatore

Then suddenly I was falling, dropping the ten feet back to the pavement. I landed hard, but not horribly—nothing was broken. Nothing, save the fabric of my shirt, which had torn away where Asbeel had held it, dropping me to the ground and leaving the airborne demon holding a shred of cloth.

The demon swooped in, but Perrault was there, fending it off with his stiletto. He grabbed me, picked me up, and turned to run. But again the demon was in his way, cutting off all retreat. With no other option, Perrault turned on his heel and sprinted down the nearest wharf.

He set me down and turned to face Asbeel, who landed behind us and was approaching, his obsidian staff pointed at us.

No, not at us, I realized. It was pointed at the dock in front of us.

The pier burst into unnatural, magical flame, leaping twenty feet in the air and spreading wide. The flames cut off the dock and billowed out, hovering over the water. The blaze was massive and intense and didn't subside, even as the wood beneath it was consumed.

Perrault pushed me behind him to guard me from the demon. He readied his stiletto and made a snapping motion with his wrist, as if to throw it, but he didn't let go. The movement seemed to roll along the blade, extending it, until the dagger turned into a sword, a thin and fine blade slightly curved at the end, sharp as glass and beautifully crafted. Perrault held it vertically in front of him and set his feet, one in front of the other, the rear foot turned sideways. With his left arm, he swept back his glorious blue cloak and he looked impressive, heroic, unbeatable.

The terrible demon stepped through the wall of fire, completely immune to the blaze, looking taller, fiercer, and more evil than ever. Before that monster, the man who was as my father looked puny indeed.

The demon no longer carried the obsidian staff. In its place he held a sword. As fine and beautiful as Perrault's bright saber appeared, the demon's blade was the perfect opposite. Black iron, the blade was longer than Perrault was tall, and the whole length of it curved. The convex edge, the sharp side, was wickedly serrated, with bright red barbs lining its length. Even the hilt looked capable of killing. Its crosspiece of twisted metal spikes, a dozen perhaps, jutted at odd angles, and several more spikes stuck out beneath the demon's red hand where a pommel should have been. More frightening still, the length of the blade blazed with red flame.

Asbeel glared at Perrault, his malicious grin gone. "Your blade is far too fine for such a weakling to wield," he growled. Perrault, still in his fencing pose, brought his blade up to his forehead and snapped it down again in a sarcastic salute.

Asbeel wasted no time setting himself, nor trading cautious jabs to take a measure of his foe. Instead, he charged at Perrault, beating his massive red wings once to create an impressive burst of momentum. The sword swung down with brutal force.

Perrault was ready for him, and knowing Asbeel's unearthly strength, he wisely didn't block the attack. Instead, he stepped toward the blade, ducking low and using his own weapon to divert the flaming sword over his head.

Asbeel overbalanced as his swing met no resistance, and Perrault, his feet solidly set and his balance perfectly centered, lunged forward. He couldn't bring his blade to bear, but punched out with the hilt of his sword instead, jamming his pommel into Asbeel's eye. The demon's head snapped back violently.

Asbeel staggered backward a step and beat his wings, thrusting himself away from Perrault. Perrault brought his blade to bear and lurched ahead. As he lunged, Perrault's own rapier burst into flame—a blue flame, not red like Asbeel's. Perrault's radiated chilling cold, not heat.

The demon's eyes widened. Realizing he could not back up far enough to avoid it, he took the only defense left—he fell to the ground, dropping hard onto the dock.

A light mist rose up around him, as if his presence so close to the water offended the river, and it was responding with fog.

Perrault was at full extension, his back leg

R.A. & Geno Salvatore

straight out behind him and his forward arm locked in front. He was able to quickly regain his defensive position, but he was unable to press the attack before Asbeel scrambled away, rising to his feet and bringing his sword up.

The demon glared at Perrault, the hatred in his eyes mixed with newfound respect. He raised his blade, holding it horizontal to his body, and approached more cautiously.

The mist continued to rise and thicken, and I could see only the dim outline of Perrault as he fended off the demon. Their movements seemed slow, ethereal. I didn't feel as though I was watching a sword fight, but a slow dance, each participant moving in harmony, action and reaction and action again.

But the brilliant light of the flaming blades wasn't dimmed by the fog, and the speed of the swings wasn't slowed. As the swords cut and slashed, each time I felt as though a hit was inevitable, and each time I held my breath. And each time, the swords passed harmlessly or were parried successfully.

The Stowaway

Then Asbeel changed his grip and reversed his direction, stepping forward and swinging his sword from low to high instead of high to low. Perrault was unable to step into the parries and under the sword. Instead, he had to leap out of the way, first to his left, then to his right. Blue flame crashed against red, and the clang of metal mixed with the angry hiss of fire on ice.

On the third swing, Perrault stepped straight back, leaning on his rear foot as the fiery blade swept just in front of him. For a moment, I thought the blade would hit him, and I nearly screamed—but the hellish red flame did not quite reach.

Perrault settled all his weight on his back foot, set firmly on the ground, his blade forward and ready. Asbeel, off balance, his sword out wide, had no defense. Perrault lunged, viciously, brutally, his sword tip reaching the five feet to Asbeel in the blink of an eye. The demon tried to fall back, to step aside, to get out of the way of that cold steel blade. But the motion was too fast, too fluid, too perfect, and the demon had nowhere to go.

The sword struck Asbeel in the chest and drove into a lung. Asbeel's howl of agony became a gurgle as blood surged from his mouth. The cold fire burned into his flesh, hissing wickedly.

In desperation, Asbeel brought his sword around hilt-first, but Perrault reversed his previous motion, retracting the blade and retreating a step, falling back into his fighting stance, at the ready.

"You are outmatched, demon," said Perrault. His voice showed not the least bit of fear. "Leave now and never return, or I shall destroy you."

Asbeel laughed.

"I think there may be a better way," the demon said. His baritone voice sounded slightly wet as blood choked his words.

He looked directly at me. I found myself staring into those fiery points of light where his eyes should have been. I tried, but I couldn't pull my gaze away, couldn't shut my eyes, couldn't move at all.

A voice sounded in my head—Asbeel's voice, but deeper, louder. *Come to me,* it said, and I found myself moving, crawling along the wharf toward Asbeel.

I tried to resist—oh, how I wanted to resist!—but I couldn't. My mind screamed, *Stop moving! Run away!* But my body refused to obey. It just kept crawling toward my doom. I felt disjointed, unattached to anything, as if I were simply an observer looking through eyes that had been mine. I saw tears well up in my eyes but I couldn't feel them as they ran down my cheeks. I saw my hands moving rhythmically, one in front of the other, pulling me along.

Perrault leaped in front of me, and he was saying something, but I could hear none of it. All I heard was that terrible voice, echoing in my skull: *Come to me.*

Then Perrault's cloak, that beautiful magical cloak, was flying around us. As it descended over me, the voice died.

I felt like myself again. I felt wet, and hot, and more than a little embarrassed, but I *felt.*

When Perrault rose, spinning to face the demon, I realized the cost of his action.

R.A. & Geno Salvatore

As soon as Perrault turned his back on Asbeel, the demon began moving. The horrible red sword descended.

It caught Perrault on the left shoulder and tore down, scratching across his chest, tearing a great gash, ripping at his skin and burning his flesh. Perrault staggered backward, one unsteady step after another, then he fell flat on his back.

"Now you die, foolish man, and I claim what is mine by right," cackled the demon.

"It is not yours, foul one. The stone chooses the wielder, and it has chosen the boy." There was strength in Perrault's voice, though he lay unmoving on the dock. The mist briefly swirled away from him, revealing his face—a bit pale, but smiling. "You can never use it, and you know it."

The demon laughed. "I was not talking about the *stone*, fool. I was talking about the *boy*. The boy I found, the boy I orphaned, the boy whose soul belongs to me." Asbeel coughed and spat out a mouthful of blood then he stepped toward Perrault, who lay still, barely keeping his grip on his sword.

"The boy's soul is his own," Perrault growled

back, his anger matching Asbeel's. "You cannot use the stone through him unless he chooses to help you, which I find doubtful."

Asbeel laughed again. He beat his wings and threw himself at Perrault. Suddenly, the scene was crystal clear. The fog vanished, disappearing so quickly that I wondered if it had ever truly been there.

Time seemed to slow down. Asbeel hung in the air, his blade arcing toward Perrault, who had raised his sword above himself in a feeble defense. Over the hills just visible in the east, the top of the sun had risen over the clouds on the horizon, its light sparkling off the city and the river.

Above the demon, breaking through the wall of fire, came an object white and sleek: a magnificent horse, her eyes glowing with white light, her mane glistening in the suddenly-brilliant sunlight.

Haze burst through the flames in all her glory. Her head smashed into the demon's back and Asbeel was launched off the end of the dock.

He tried to beat his wings, but only one responded. The other, which had taken the brunt

R.A. & Geno Salvatore

of Haze's charge, was twisted and broken.

Like an injured bird, the demon plummeted into the river, disappearing beneath the waves without a sound.

"He will be back," Perrault said, his voice low and full of pain. "But not soon."

With great effort, he pulled himself to a sitting position and reached into one of Haze's saddlebags. Out came a long white bandage and a vial of oil. He poured the oil onto the cloth then wrapped it tightly around his chest, trying to stem the flow of blood from his gory wound.

From behind us I heard a sharp crack, like lightning striking a tree, and a splash. A section of the burning dock collapsed into the river.

"Come. Let's get out of here," Perrault said. He managed to pull himself up into Haze's saddle. I followed, taking my seat behind him.

"Our way is blocked," I said.

"Only one way," came the response. "There are others." And with that, Haze wheeled around and took off at a gallop—directly off the end of the pier.

Chapter Sixteen

As we hit the ocean, the waves rose up around us, but they did not slow Haze's speed. She ran up and down over the cresting water. The jarring motion sent my stomach reeling. I was afraid I might vomit, though thankfully I had not eaten anything since the night before.

I pressed my face tightly against Perrault's back, and after a while, I lifted my head to look around. I should have done so much sooner. The sun was uncomfortably warm on my head, but the salty ocean wind felt cool.

I noticed Perrault held Haze's reins with only his right hand, despite our swift pace. The sight upset my stomach even more than the cresting waves.

I swallowed. "Are you sure your shoulder is all right, sir?"

"Maimun, do not pester me with your questions right now." Perrault said. But I could hear the pain in his voice. "Close your eyes. We have a long journey ahead."

I did as I was told. The sounds, the smells, and the feeling of that glorious wind swept over me, and soon all thoughts of my tossing stomach were lost—along with my sense of time. I couldn't say how long we rode before Haze came to a stop.

I opened my eyes to a magnificent sight: a ship had grown from the ocean in front of us!

I had seen ships before, but mostly in the distance—even the ones on the river at Baldur's Gate—but I had never seen one up close. The sheer size of the mighty vessel staggered me. It must have been a hundred feet long! It moved across the great flat plain of the ocean with impressive

R.A. & Geno Salvatore

speed, and Haze had to run to keep up with it. I studied the deck and the massive square sails. I watched, my mouth hanging open, as the great sheets of white furled upward, seeming to rise of their own free will, and the ship slowed.

A dozen sailors stood at the rail. Their expressions mirrored my own, mouths hanging open, eyes wide, and it took me a moment to realize what they were staring at. Then it hit me: The ship they stood upon, for all its size, was *supposed* to be there. The horse on which Perrault and I rode was not.

Another man joined the crew at the rail. I knew he must be the captain, for he was well dressed—or would have been, if his clothing hadn't been so old. The blue jacket he wore must have once been covered with ornaments, but all that remained was one brass button and loose golden threads. Upon his head sat a dusty hat much decorated in brass. It had a strange shape, almost flat, with corners sticking out far to the sides of his head. A tassel of the same golden thread as his bandolier hung down on each side of the hat. He would have looked like a gentleman, even a noble, except his

The Stowaway

brown hair was wild and untrimmed, and the look in his eye was just as wild.

"Give me one reason not to have you killed where you ride," the captain called down. He had the voice of a street thug, coarse and harsh, but with the inflection and pronunciation of an educated man.

"We've given you no reason to attack, good sir," Perrault replied.

"That devil horse is reason aplenty, I'm thinking! It ain't natural, a horse ridin' on the waves!" As he spoke, he grew visibly and audibly agitated, and the other sailors at the rail bristled and nodded their agreement.

"Devil?" Perrault replied. "Hardly. Angelic, more like! I come as an emissary from the Temple of Tymora at Baldur's Gate. If you attack us, you shan't be allowed back in that city, which"—he looked deliberately at the front of the ship—"is your port of call, judging by your flag."

Perrault was lying. Even if I hadn't known we were not such emissaries, I could hear the lie in his voice. I hoped the sailors could not.

154

The men seemed suddenly less comfortable, and the captain stuttered several times before he managed to respond.

"Prove it, then! I ain't heared o' no emissary o' no temple comin' out 'cross the water on a damned horse afore, an' I ain't been told o' nobody lookin' for my ship. So prove it, or we'll kill ye as ye ride!" Any semblance of dignity had left his voice—he sounded every bit the salty seafarer.

Perrault reached into one of the pouches on Haze's saddle and pulled out a rolled piece of parchment. "A message from the temple, for your eyes only, Captain," he called.

"Oy, toss it up then."

Perrault obliged—almost. He threw the parchment at the captain, but it didn't quite reach his hands. Its momentum seemed to die about three feet from the rail. The captain reached out for the parchment, leaning out a bit too far. A sudden gust of wind caught him full in the back and he tumbled right over the rail, dropping with a splash into the water beside us.

The Stowaway

He came up, gasping and choking. His hat floated beside him, but even as he reached for it, the heavy brass weighed it down and the object disappeared from sight.

The captain struggled just to stay afloat. Haze wheeled around, and Perrault grabbed the man's arm and held him. Perrault couldn't lift the man, but kept his head above the water, and as Haze trotted along beside the moving ship, the captain was pulled with us.

"Oy, what're ye waitin' fer!" he screamed at the crewmen on the rail, who were staring at us in shock. "Drop us a damned launch, ye fools!" The men ran from the rail and soon returned with a rowboat on ropes and pulleys, which they began to lower into the water.

Before the boat was halfway down the side of the ship, the captain ripped his hand away from Perrault and *jumped*. Somehow, he pushed the entire upper half of his body from the water, despite having nothing to brace against, no footing, and a heavy, soaked coat weighing him down.

He sputtered and stuttered and shouted, but his words were unintelligible. He began swimming furiously, trying to find a handhold on the side of the ship, but there were none, so he screamed at the men above.

"The launch! Lower the damned launch! It just brushed my foot—it just . . . damned shark! There's a damned shark in the water and it . . . There it is again! Get that boat in the water!"

The men hastened to obey their captain at the word *shark*. In a matter of seconds, the launch reached the water—mostly because two of the crewmen lost their grips on the ropes in their haste. The boat plummeted the last ten feet, narrowly missing the captain, and landed upside-down.

The captain seemed unconcerned with the graceless landing, and hardly seemed to notice the boat wasn't right. He quickly climbed up onto the keel of the small craft and yelled up for a rope.

Again, the crew responded with speed but not grace—a coil of rope was thrown down. The crewman who threw it had fine aim, it seemed—the rope caught the captain square on the forehead, knocking him off his feet. Somehow, he stayed on the boat, despite the lack of handholds and the rounded surface. He seemed afraid that even touching the water would mean a painful death, and his fear lent him acrobatic talents he could not normally command.

The captain didn't even berate the sailor for his errant throw. He simply grabbed the rope and hauled himself up, hand over hand, with remarkable speed. Once he reached the top, he turned and called down to us, "Are you coming, or shall I haul the rope up?"

"Neither, and both," Perrault replied. Haze trotted beside the overturned launch and Perrault grabbed one side of it, flipping it over easily. Then Haze stepped into the launch, and Perrault hopped off the horse. I followed suit. He took the rope and tied it to the boat. "Toss us three more ropes, then haul them all up when we're set."

The captain offered a nod, then walked from the rail. The crewmen threw three more ropes and we tied them to the boat. The light craft groaned in protest at the weight of the horse, but it held strong, as did the pulleys—and the men working them—on deck.

Barely a moment later, Perrault and I were in the captain's cabin, the door shutting behind us with a soft click.

Chapter Seventeen

The captain's cabin was richly furnished with a thick red carpet, many cabinets, and small tables of fine dark wood—all bolted to the walls or the floor. Dozens of knick-knacks lay scattered around the room: here an ancient oil lamp of tarnished brass, there a finely crafted tea kettle and four cups inside a locked cabinet with a glass door, and over there—hanging above the other door to the cabin—a strange object with a wooden handle and a long metal tube. It looked very much like a drawing of a thing called an arquebus I had once seen in a book titled *Unusual Armaments*.

The captain sat comfortably on a worn chair behind an enormous table, on which lay heaps of papers—notes, charts of the stars, maps of varying scale detailing the sea from Waterdeep in the north to Calimport in the south. Apparently he had a spare hat, identical to the one he'd lost, for it was atop his head as if nothing had happened. And a spare coat, it seemed, since the one covering him was dry. The only indication that he had been in the water was the puddle slowly spreading beneath his chair. I tried not to look at it, out of politeness.

The captain motioned to the two chairs opposite him.

"Please sit," he said, the saltiness of his voice hidden beneath his trained accent. "What can I do for an emissary of the Temple of Tymora?" I heard a note of sarcasm, and surely Perrault did as well, but he ignored it.

"That depends largely on the course you've set," replied Perrault.

"We make for Luskan with all haste, to sell

R.A. & Geno Salvatore

our cargo and refill our holds, that we might leave for the south before the ice of winter traps us in port."

Perrault sat silently for a moment, hand on chin, deep in thought. "Then what you can do for us, good Captain . . ."

"Smythe," said the man. Perrault nodded.

"What you can do, Captain Smythe, is divert your course to Waterdeep. I have business there of the utmost urgency."

Captain Smythe scowled, but only for a moment before he caught himself. "If we make for Waterdeep, we shan't make Luskan in time to load and head south, so we'd have to sell and buy in Waterdeep instead. The prices will not be as high, and the goods we take on there shall be of lesser quality. So tell me, will the temple compensate me for this loss?"

Perrault only smiled. "The temple's compensation comes in the form of the flag you now fly."

Captain Smythe didn't even try to hide his scowl. "The loss is too great. I cannot agree."

"You would deny an emissary of the—"

"I never saw proof that you are from the temple!"

"Only because you dropped the parchment." Perrault's tone was mocking, insulting.

Smythe stood up, his voice rising with him. "I dropped it because you threw it so poorly!"

Perrault stood, matching the captain's intensity. "You asked that it be thrown, instead of inviting us aboard! You threatened to kill us without proof, then when proof was offered— *you* demanded it be thrown. And you dropped it. Deliberately, I say! You dropped it so you wouldn't have to recognize my authority!"

Captain Smythe's hand moved to his sword, but Perrault was faster. In the blink of an eye, his fine stiletto was in hand, pointed at the captain.

Smythe stopped and took his hand off his sword. "Regardless, I will not divert my course without some proof of your claim or a promise of compensation." He sat down, and after a moment, Perrault did as well. "But I will allow you to sail with us. I will even offer you the comfort of my own cabin for the journey, and free run of

R.A. & Geno Salvatore

the ship until we reach Luskan. It is not far from there to Waterdeep. It will take only five days' sailing or maybe a tenday's ride. That's the best I can offer you."

Perrault nodded. "Very well. Though the temple will not be pleased to hear of my treatment."

"A risk I must take," replied Captain Smythe. "Now, if you will excuse me, I must see to the crew. Please, make yourselves comfortable."

Chapter Eighteen

As soon as I was sure Smythe had gone, I turned to Perrault. "You aren't an emissary from any temple," I whispered. "You lied to him."

"Repeatedly and continuously, and for his own good," Perrault answered. He leaned back in his chair and gazed up at the ceiling of the captain's small cabin. His shirt had come untucked and I caught a glimpse of the stark white bandage wrapped around his chest.

"But lying is bad," I said.

"So I was bad." Perrault stood up and circled

the captain's desk. He picked up one of the maps and studied it intently. "And I didn't even get what I wanted, did I? We're still sailing for Luskan, but we need to be off this boat a good deal sooner."

I shook my head, not understanding. "What was on the parchment you threw to him, anyway?"

"Absolutely nothing," he replied without looking up from the map. "It was blank."

"So if he had caught it, what would have happened?"

"Many bad things." He set the map down on the desk and looked at me with that familiar twinkle in his eye. "The captain probably would have ordered us killed, and then I would have had to take the ship myself, one against dozens. It might have taken an hour to accomplish!" He began to laugh then stopped abruptly. He held his arm against the wound on his chest, flexing against the pain. "Perhaps two hours, with this gash slowing me down. And then we would have had to sail this ship to Waterdeep all by ourselves. Trust me, that is no easy feat!"

I would have been laughing, surely, but the

pain on his face when he clutched at the wound sobered me.

"You threw the parchment so he couldn't catch it, didn't you?" I asked, the picture coming clear. "Then you said *he* dropped it deliberately, so he wouldn't be able to accuse you of the same thing!"

Perrault bowed slightly. "Precisely."

"And the wind," I said. "Did you conjure that wind to knock him off the ship?"

"You overestimate me. That was fortuitous coincidence."

"Fortui . . . what?"

"Fortuitous, like fortune. Luck. That was lucky chance."

"So why did the captain give us his cabin?" I had seen Perrault get whatever he wanted with merely a well-worded question, but the cabin had been offered up, not asked for—and that immediately following a near sword fight!

"Etiquette." I opened my mouth, but Perrault held up his hand to stop me. "Etiquette . . . manners. When a distinguished guest is aboard the ship, the captain is supposed to offer his cabin.

The Stowaway

He probably has a spare cabin below made up and ready for him for just such occasions."

"But he didn't believe you. He doesn't think you're a distinguished guest."

"He's hedging his bets. He refuses to obey my request, because he doesn't think I work for the people I claim to represent. But to not offer me his cabin, if I were telling the truth, would be a tremendous insult. This way, if he's wrong, I can tell my superiors that he didn't obey, but he wasn't rude. And if he's right, all he's lost is a small amount of comfort for the journey."

I was nodding before he even finished, seeing the logic. "But why do we need to trouble him, anyway?"

"I have business in Waterdeep. You heard me tell as much to the captain."

"What kind of business?" I laid my hand over my heart, feeling the lump that was the stone against my chest. "Business with this stone? Why is it so important? What does it do?"

"Enough." The finality of the word and the weight of his tone stopped my next question in my

R.A. & Geno Salvatore

throat. He crossed the small cabin to the door in a few strides. "I must see to Haze. You must sleep. I can see in your eyes that you are tired."

"I'm not tired!" I shouted back at him.

But he was already gone.

I moved to the other door, which predictably opened into the captain's sleeping quarters. The room was much more sparsely furnished, with only a cot and a dresser. I moved to the cot and flopped down atop the neatly tucked blankets.

I lay there for a while staring at the cabin's ceiling, my hands clenched at my sides. Perrault still treated me like the day he had found me under the pine boughs, the day I was six years old. He must think I was too foolish, too weak to know the truth. Even after the fight with the demon and our race across the sea—all of that, and still Perrault wouldn't see fit to trust me with the answers I most wanted to know.

Chapter Nineteen

I awoke to the sounds of movement and a clamor from above. Light streamed in through the small round window. The sun had still been up when I fell onto the cot, and it was up again now. I must have slept as the dead! My stomach ached—it had been so long since I'd last eaten. Or perhaps it ached due to the constant toss and roll of the ship. Either way, I figured food would do me well.

Perrault was not in the room, but since I was under the covers and my traveling gear was neatly piled beside the bed, I assumed he must have come to tuck me in. I rose, dressed, and walked into the outer chamber of the captain's suite.

As out of place as Haze had appeared the previous day, running along the ocean swells, she seemed even more out of place kneeling in the captain's private room. She leaned gently against a bookcase. Her head lolled as the ship rocked, and she whinnied softly. I could not tell if she was enjoying the ride, or if she was about to vomit. Fearing the latter, I skipped by, pausing just long enough to run my hand through her fine mane, and walked out onto the deck.

About half the sun peeked above the eastern horizon. There used to be land there, I thought. The sun appeared huge, more massive than I had ever seen. Its brilliant rays caught the spray off the cresting waves and lit the drops like crystals. The air felt alive with light, and the deep blue sea danced beneath it. I stood staring for a long while, until the bottom edge of the sun passed the horizon and the magic in the air faded.

I thought of what lay ahead. At least, for once, I knew where Perrault was taking us:

R.A. & Geno Salvatore

Waterdeep, the Jewel of the North, the greatest city of the Sword Coast. Baldur's Gate had been impressive—Waterdeep would be amazing. And demon-free.

It was early, but every crewmember was on deck. Some were moving about, securing this rope or moving that line, some were on hands and knees pushing a heavy horse-hair brush across the deck to clean it.

I climbed the narrow ladder to the aft deck. A few sailors stood there at the wheel, plotting a course. I crept past them to find Perrault leaning heavily against the rail, facing west.

"Sir," I said as I approached him. "I'm sorry for shouting at you last night."

He didn't reply. Standing beside him, I could hear that he was singing under his breath. I knew better than to interrupt him. I would have to find him again later, I thought. I slipped away and climbed back down to the main deck.

There Captain Smythe called out orders. "Raise the mainsail!" he shouted. Above him, climbing amid the rigging, were the lightest and most agile of the crew, shinnying along cross-beams to unfurl the sails.

The wind blew from almost directly behind us, and as soon as the men dropped the lines, mighty white sheets billowed out. The sails caught so much of the wind that I could actually feel the ship lurch forward, moving at a great clip.

High above all that activity, a girl about the same age as me stood perched in a large wooden bucket fixed to the mainmast. She had long hair the color of wheat whipping about her head.

White and gray seagulls circled her, and whenever she held out an arm, one would swoop in to land on it. She would hand the bird a small piece of bread and the gull would take off. Occasionally, she would turn to the aft deck—to the captain—and yell something. She spoke the common tongue, but with the wind and the sails, I couldn't understand a word she said.

I watched her for some time, fascinated by the gulls. I tried to keep track of them, and before long I was convinced of it: The same gull never landed on her arm twice in a row.

R.A. & Geno Salvatore

Watching the gulls feed made my stomach growl, so I headed back to the narrow ladder to find Perrault.

But before I even made it to the deck, a sailor approached me. He tipped his head, motioning to the aft deck where Perrault stood. "Your friend there said to give you this when you woke." The sailor handed me a cloth wrapped around a hunk of bread and a small piece of cheese.

I found a place against the railing, in a patch of shade. The bread was a bit stale and the cheese was too sharp—but after a full day without food, it was enough to satisfy my rumbling belly. I devoured my meal then lay back on the deck and closed my eyes.

I listened to the captain as he barked orders, and to the cawing of the gulls, and to the splash of the ocean waves against the hull of the ship. The sounds mixed so well they seemed to become one, a perfect harmonious rhythm, the song of the sea, I thought.

The previous day had been horrible; today could only be an improvement. Perrault's wound would be on the mend. Asbeel would be farther away.

But in the back of my mind, questions nagged at me. What if Perrault got worse? What if Asbeel found us on the ship? Dark thoughts crowded my head, but I didn't even try to shake them.

"Oy, you awake, kid?" It was the girl from the crow's nest, poking me.

"No," I said without opening my eyes.

She smirked. "Then how are you talking, eh?"

"I talk in my sleep all the time. Just ask Perrault."

"Who's that, then?" she asked.

I knew I was being rude, but I couldn't help myself. The last thing I wanted to do was make small talk with a girl. I sat up and stared at her. "Perrault's the guy I came here with." I filled my voice with as much venom as I was capable of. "You think a kid like me could make it here all alone?"

"I didn't think a kid could make it here at all," she said. "You weren't here when we set off from the Gate. And I ain't recallin' us stoppin' to pick you up! How did you get here, eh?"

R.A. & Geno Salvatore

"Perrault and I rode. How else could we have come?" I said it as if it was so obvious, as if there were no other choice, but of course that made no sense. How could someone *ride* to a ship, particularly across the open sea?

She just rolled her eyes at me and smirked. "So he's your father, then?"

I was shaking my head before she finished. "No. He's just . . . He's . . ." What was he, I wondered. Surely Perrault was the closest thing I had to a father, and he cared for me and protected me as a parent should, yet when she asked that question . . .

"Say no more. You're an orphan, ain't ya?" She smiled again, but this time there was only gentleness there, so I abandoned my planned response—spittle—and just nodded. "An orphan, just like me. Name's Joen. What're you called, then?"

"Maimun." I could barely get the word out—a orphan, just like me, she'd said. Something about the sound of that word, leveled at me by someone other than Asbeel, shook me up. I'd never thought of myself as an orphan, though of course I was. I had always had someone, and even if Elbeth and Perrault weren't my parents by birth, they surely were by deed.

"Well then, Maimun. Wanna come with me? I'll show you 'round the ship, eh?"

I shrugged. "I guess so." I had nothing better to do while I waited for Perrault.

Joen led me around the ship, and pointed out each detail. The foredeck had a carving of a mermaid out front she called a "figurehead." Joen said we could have climbed out there, if the boat wasn't moving so fast. She showed me the crew's quarters, with the galley behind, where we swiped a loaf of bread. Then the hold, full of wool, dried fruit, and pottery from the Heartlands for trade in the North.

When we made it back to the deck, the captain was looking for Joen, wearing an angry scowl that seemed so at home on his grizzled face. But as soon as he saw me, his expression tightened.

"Joen, quit your playing, your break's over.

Get up in the crow's nest before I have you whipped."

Joen lowered her eyes and nodded, moving toward the mainmast. I followed close behind. She tucked the loaf of bread into her belt and began scaling the mast—it was set with pegs specifically for that purpose, I could see—but she stopped a few rungs up. "Oy, ya wanna join me in the crow's nest?" she asked.

I hesitated. I had been rude to this girl, this fellow orphan, had all but told her to leave. But she had not, and was even asking me to join her. Asking me as a friend? I had never had a friend—save Perrault—and I realized I wouldn't know what to look for in one. Or maybe she was just planning to drop some of her work on me?

"Hurry up!" she called over her shoulder.

Worth finding out her intentions, I decided.

"Shouldn't this place be called the gull's nest?" I asked as I set my foot on the first rung. "Those birds aren't crows, they're gulls!"

Joen smiled widely. "All right, come join me in the gull's nest, then."

The Stowaway

We spent the rest of the day up among the birds. I had never been so high in the air, and the view was dazzling.

I leaned over the side of the tiny bucket, and saw the sailors milling around on the deck. "They look as small as halflings." I laughed.

I stared down at the little people on the big ship and imagined they were oversized rodents, scurrying about from hole to hole, as they appeared and disappeared among the massive sails, the holds, and the many nooks not visible to a person from above. I made up a story on the spot about a rat who wished to become a sailor and the captain who made that dream come true. I told my tale to Joen in my best imitation of Perrault's storytelling voice.

When I finished, she clapped. "You should come up here every day," she said. "This ship's a whole lot more interesting with you aboard. Where did you hear that tale?"

"I made it up, just now. I guess one day I

R.A. & Geno Salvatore

. . . well, . . . maybe I might like to learn to be a sailor, too."

"Here's your first lesson, then," Joen caught my hand and pointed it to the east. "Do you see the land there?"

I shook my head. To every side, the horizon appeared perfectly flat.

"Look harder! If you wanna work the crow's— I mean, *gull's* nest, you gotta keep a sharp eye out for anything." Joen jabbed my hand, tracing a line. "See? The color of the horizon is different out there, darker."

I squinted, and a line of gray came into focus atop the shining blue sea. "I can see it!"

"And there, moving parallel to us in the west—" She whipped me around and pointed my arm at the other side. "Sails! See them?"

The sun was bright and the horizon hazy, but I could just make out a speck of white riding the edge of the sea. I nodded.

Joen laughed. "You're a natural, then! I gotta lot a stuff I could show you. Tell your father— or whatever you call him—that you wanna stay

aboard. Maybe the captain'd give him a job or something, eh?"

I shrugged. "We have to leave at Luskan." My stomach twisted and I remembered the argument Perrault and I had had the night before.

Joen picked up the loaf of bread from the floor of the crow's nest and ripped off a piece. "Well, maybe you can come back some day." She held out the piece of bread and a gull swooped out of nowhere to land on her arm. The bird gobbled it up in one bite, then dropped off her arm, wings outstretched. I followed his flight until I lost sight of him on the horizon. How would it feel to be so free?

When we ran out of bread, the gulls circled a bit longer before swooping off. They dropped into the ship's wake, skimming off the waves. Joen explained that the cook would be preparing the night's meal, and his scraps would be tossed out a porthole. The gulls would scavenge it all. Their appetites were infinite, it seemed.

After what seemed like hours, the thin clouds lit up, flaring brilliant red, as did the sea. The sun

descended into its own shimmering reflection, orange meeting orange, and it seemed rather than setting, the sun was collapsing on itself.

"Wait till you see this." Joen smiled at me. "You ain't seen a sunset until you've seen a sunset at sea."

I had always loved to watch colors explode across the sky, orange, pink, red, and sometimes even a regal violet, but somehow this was different and not just because I was at sea. As the sun dipped lower, a shadow spread across the ocean to the east, coming from the land toward the ship like some great dark wave. As it reached the ship, I watched as the shadow climbed up the side, then onto the deck, then slowly up the mainmast.

When the shadow touched us in the gull's nest, the sun disappeared from sight. On the eastern horizon, the stars were already twinkling, growing brighter and more numerous by the second.

"I gotta get down to the galley and help Cook." Joen put her foot down on the mainmast's top peg and began to descend. "But maybe I'll see you around the gull's nest again."

The Stowaway

I watched as she headed below then followed her down. At the bottom, I rushed to the eastern rail of the ship. I had seen sunrise then sunset at sea; now I intended to see the stars' bright lights. The night sky always seemed darker when few lights were about, like the open countryside. On the sea, there was no light save the tiny beacon at the bow of the ship. I stood transfixed for a good while, counting the stars as they appeared, trying to identify constellations and individual heavenly bodies.

I tried to remember the lessons I'd learned about navigating by the night sky, to figure out where we were and where we were heading.

After a time, Perrault joined me. "You missed the meal," he said. "So I brought you some." He handed me a plate of hard biscuits and salted meat.

I took the food gratefully, but could only nibble. Instead, I gulped deeply at the sights and sounds of the ship, and the salty smell of the sea.

Perrault stayed by my side for a moment, gently cradling his left arm and gazing out at the

R.A. & Geno Salvatore

sea. He slipped away after only a moment, saying something as he went. It might have been, "Don't stay out too late," but I couldn't tell.

I couldn't say how long I stared out across the sea, first at the east rail, then at the west. All my favorite constellations were either west or south of the ship that time of year.

But some time later, a tiny speck on the horizon caught my eye. It was so small that it could have been the reflection of the stars off the water, except it didn't waver with the waves. At first I wasn't sure if I was imagining it. Perhaps I had spent too long staring at the stars. I closed my eyes and listened to the waves against the boat, the creaking of the wood, the low howl of the wind. I breathed deeply then I opened my eyes and scanned our ship.

Only two lanterns were lit, one at the prow and one at the stern, and a single lookout stood near each lantern, gazing out inattentively. My eyes swept back out to sea, along the horizon, and there it was again.

The tiny fleck didn't move at all—except, I noticed after a short time, it appeared to be

The Stowaway

growing. More to the point, it was *closing*. I realized with a shock that it was a ship. And it was coming right at us.

R.A. & Geno Salvatore

Chapter Twenty

I let out a gasp as I backed off the rail, unsure
what to do. Perrault was asleep, surely, and he had
told me not to be out too late—what time was it?
If I woke him, and it was nothing, he would know
I had disobeyed, and I would be punished. But if I
did nothing, and the ship was heading to attack,
the consequences would be worse. So I settled for
the middle path. I had to alert somebody, just not
Perrault. I rushed to find the forward lookout.

"Wake up! Wake up, sir," I said. He didn't
answer, so I repeated my request more forcefully,

accentuating it with a push. He responded with a loud snore, and an empty bottle tumbled out from its cradle in the crook of his arm. He would be no help.

Frustrated, I ran to the stern and climbed up on the aft deck near the ship's wheel. The guard was awake, but when I rushed over, he spoke in a language I didn't understand.

" 'Ey boy, 'ows enyt trit'n or ees?" he said through a mouth devoid of teeth. My blank stare prompted a repetition, but the words came no more clearly.

I decided to speak to him and hope he could understand me. "Sir, there's something out there," I said, pointing to the western horizon.

"O ah, der sum'n ery ware, ya know, boy," he replied with a kind-hearted smile. Again, I couldn't make any sense of the words.

"A ship is out there, coming directly at us. It's closing fast. I don't know what to do!" I pronounced every word very clearly, and this time it seemed to sink in. The kindly smile disappeared from his face, replaced by a look of fear.

R.A. & Geno Salvatore

"A chip?"

"A ship. Yes. Right there." I moved to the rail and pointed straight at it. The man followed me, and stared into the darkness.

He fell back from the rail and sounded the alarm.

"A chip! A chip! Cap'n, wek de Cap'n, ders a chip an its lik'n be'n pirates! Pirates, Cap'n!" he screamed loudly as he rushed to the ladder and down, toward the cabin Perrault and I had taken. Realizing his error, he galloped below decks. I could hear his screams echoing up from below. The only word he could pronounce clearly was "pirates," and I heard it over and over, each time sending a chill up my spine.

Soon the deck was a flurry of activity, men scrambling all around. Many went up the mainmast to unfurl the sails, sure-handed even in the darkness. The helmsman, the captain, and Perrault all made their way to the aft deck, where I stood. Anyone without a task gathered at the west rail, watching the ship as it closed.

As soon as the sails were unfurled, they were

The Stowaway

turned to catch the wind, but the wind blew in from the west, from starboard, and though we could catch a fair breeze, our pursuer had it full on her back. Soon we were turning, running in a straight line with the pursuer. But still the ship closed.

"We cannot outpace her, Captain, she runs too swiftly," I heard Perrault say quietly, so none of the crew would overhear. "We should consider surrendering."

The captain's face turned red. "You have no authority to make such a decision. I say we run, and we hope at dawn to see friendly sails to deter the pirates! And if not, we'll deter them ourselves, at sword point!" The captain's voice was loud, and several nearby crew turned to look. A few let out a halfhearted cheer at the captain's proclamation.

"If you run," Perrault replied, lifting his voice to match the captain's, "and are caught, they will be far less merciful. If you fight, they will slaughter you, every one." No cheers at that, but a few of the sailors nodded in agreement. The captain's face was turning toward purple.

R.A. & Geno Salvatore

"Are you telling me," Smythe said, straining to keep his tone level, "to surrender my ship, to entrust the fate of myself and my crew to the mercy of pirates?"

"My own fate, and that of my ward, are tied to yours."

"Not so long as you have that damned horse!" He was screaming and the crew stared, but Smythe didn't notice. "I'll kill the thing, and then we'll see if you want to surrender!"

He took a step toward the captain's cabin, where Haze was resting. But only one step, because suddenly Perrault was armed, his sword pointed at the captain's throat. "You have but one more step to take, sir. Choose it wisely."

Smythe turned slowly to face Perrault. "Get off my deck," he said.

Perrault nodded and turned to me. He took my hand, gently, and led me to the captain's quarters. All the way, I could hear a stream of curses pouring from Captain Smythe. I tried to ignore him, but it was impossible. By the time the cabin door closed behind us, I was shaking.

The Stowaway

Perrault checked on Haze—she was still exhausted from the taxing run so far out to sea. I wanted to suggest we ride away before the pirates arrived, but seeing her, I knew there was no chance. She could run forever across the ground, but running over water cost her great energy. Looking at her now, I was amazed we ever even reached the ship. I wondered if Perrault had known where the ship would be before we set off, and the thought chilled me—running blind across the great open ocean, hoping to find a ship, a mere speck on the great blue emptiness. . . .

Perrault led Haze into the captain's bedroom and I followed. He slid the heavy dresser in front of the door and stood near the porthole. I realized I was exhausted, so I dropped onto the cot. Despite my tiredness, no sleep would come. A question pressed at my mind until I could hold it no longer, so I had to ask Perrault, "What will happen when the pirates catch us?"

Perrault's expression was grim. "If the crew fight, they will die. If they surrender, who knows?"

R.A. & Geno Salvatore

Chapter Twenty~One

It was past dawn before the pirates caught us. The captain's hope of friendly sails had not come true.

Nor had his plan to fight.

Wisely, the crewmen ignored their captain's call to arms. Badly outnumbered, they laid down their weapons and hoped for mercy. The pirates were happy to oblige—the only thing better than looting a ship, after all, was looting a ship without anyone in the way.

The captain's quarters were by no means protected from the looting, and it was not long before we heard several men enter the outer room. I heard furniture skidding across the floor and small crashes as the pirates tossed items about.

I peered out the tiny crack between the door and the jamb to see a pair of pirates ransacking the place. They were dirty, filthy, covered in the grime of tendays at sea without a bath. The room lay in ruins, each piece of furniture meticulously tipped over. Parchment and shattered wood lay everywhere.

One of the men held a small horn with a leather strap. The other held the arquebus I had seen earlier. They poured smokepowder down the barrel of the oddly-shaped thing—copious amounts of it—far, far too much.

After a moment, the one holding the weapon stepped back, said something, and pointed it directly at the other man, laughing all the while. The other threw his hands up to cover his face and dived backward.

The first pirate lifted his thumb to the hammer at the base of the barrel, pulled back, and let go.

The flash blinded me, the blast deafened me,

and the ringing in my ears took a good while to fade. As I reoriented myself, I heard cursing, laughing, and shouting from the next room. The pirates had survived the blast. A shame, I thought.

Then I heard a different kind of blast—the banging of a heavy fist on the door to our barricaded little room.

"The ship's been surrendered, ye need to be lettin' us in!" came the call from outside.

"This room is off limits, good sir," Perrault replied.

"Ain't nowhere off limits! Open the door!" The banging fist was replaced by a much heavier thud as the man threw his shoulder into the door.

The door had no lock, and the barricade wasn't especially sturdy—every slam slid the dresser a few inches. It wouldn't be long before the pirate pushed through. Perrault knew this. He held his sword out—but in his left hand. His right was pressed tightly against his chest, which appeared to be bleeding again, staining his shirt.

"You err badly, sailor. Fetch your captain, and

The Stowaway

he will confirm: this room is off limits to you."
How Perrault could keep his voice so calm despite
his pain and such obvious danger amazed me. I
wanted to hide under the bed, or scramble out the
porthole, but I took courage from Perrault and
did neither. Instead I hid behind Haze, stroking
her mane to keep her quiet.

The banging at the door stopped and was
replaced by heavy, sharp footsteps. A deeper voice
spoke from behind the door.

"I seek the man called Perrault. Open this
door."

Perrault hardly seemed surprised. "Captain
Baram, I presume?"

"Indeed."

Perrault moved the barricade and opened
the door, with great effort. Standing patiently
was Captain Baram, looking every bit the pirate
and every bit the captain all at once. His clothing
was similar to Captain Smythe's outfit, but black
instead of blue. His hat was three-pointed, also
black, of old and well-worn leather. His face bore
the scars of countless battles, and his beard was

R.A. & Geno Salvatore

thicker than Smythe's, yet it looked regal, neatly trimmed, and well kept. The creases on his face spoke to years of salty ocean winds, his skin as leathery as his hat.

"Come, then, let us speak in private," said the captain. Perrault nodded, and led Haze and me out of the cabin.

On deck, the pirates had lowered two gang-planks—merely thick slabs of wood—across the gap between the ships. Baram led us across the nearer gangplank onto his ship.

We were not the only ones moving in that direction. A pair of armed pirates stood at the other plank, and a line of prisoners marched across. The crew of Captain Smythe's vessel were bound at the wrists and ankles then tied together, each to the person in front and behind. They walked with their heads down, hopeless, helpless.

At the back of one of the lines came Joen.

Her head was down, but her eyes were not. They peeked out from beneath the tangle of her hair. No fear filled those eyes, not even the resignation so visible in the older crewmen.

The Stowaway

Her roaming gaze settled upon me. She, a captive, tied to the captive in front of him, looked at me, walking free, walking behind the pirate captain himself. Joen slowed and lifted her head. The pirate guard prodded her hard with the hilt of his cutlass, but Joen didn't flinch or lower her gaze. She looked directly at me, and whispered something. And though she only whispered, and a great distance stood between us, I heard her clearly.

"I forgive you."

Forgive me for what? I wanted to shout. But Joen had already walked across the plank and out of sight, into the hold below.

Perrault tugged on my arm and I continued walking, following him and Baram to the pirate captain's quarters.

Once there, Captain Baram opened a glass cabinet—not glass, I realized, but a magical glass known as glassteel, infinitely more solid and expensive than normal glass—and withdrew a dusty bottle. He poured a thick brown liquid into two glasses then looked at me and smiled. He reached

R.A. & Geno Salvatore

for a third glass and moved as if to pour, but a look from Perrault stopped him. Captain Baram laughed and put the bottle away.

"To good health and good fortune," Baram said, raising his glass.

"Both come to those who seek it," replied Perrault, tapping his glass to the captain's.

"And to those who are shown it!" Baram replied, roaring with laughter.

"Your fortune and mine are the same. That I sought it and you found it is no coincidence."

"Ah, but only if I deliver you where you wish. I am a pirate, after all, and Waterdeep is out of my way. Why should I take you there, when it would be more profitable to return home with my new goods, and a valuable prisoner to boot?"

"Your reputation speaks otherwise, good sir."

"Indeed, indeed, and the other pirates will not cease to tease me about it!" Again came that great belly laugh, and Perrault joined in. "Very well, very well. Waterdeep it is. We should be there inside four days."

The Stowaway

Chapter Twenty~Two

Perrault seemed to know his way around the ship, and after finding shelter for Haze, he led us to an unoccupied cabin near the bow. I waited until we were alone before I allowed myself to say what I'd been thinking.

"You know the pirate captain." It was not a question—it was an accusation.

"Never met the man," Perrault replied.

"But you knew he was coming." I paced the small cabin.

"Yes." Perrault sat down on the edge of the

bed, his back turned to me.

"How did you know?"

"I called him. It was a simple spell, really, to send my voice out across the miles and tell our good Captain Baram about a ripe and cooperative take."

I stopped pacing. It took me a moment to regain enough composure to say anything. "You . . . called him?"

"I did. For good reason." Perrault loosened his traveling cloak and laid it on the bed beside him. I could see dark patches of sweat staining the back of his finely woven shirt.

"What reason?" I clenched my fists and tried not to shout.

"The captain would not divert his ship's course," Perrault said with no emotion in his voice. "We needed to be off the sea a good deal sooner than Luskan."

I covered my face with my hands. "But what about Captain Smythe's ship, and his sailors, and all their stuff? They're all captured. Joen's captured. And it's all because of us . . . because of you . . ."

R.A. & Geno Salvatore

Suddenly I knew exactly why Joen had for-given me. She knew the terrible thing that Perrault had done. My eyes began to fill with tears I didn't want Perrault to see. "If the sailors hadn't surrendered, they would have been killed. You nearly got the whole crew killed! Is getting to land sooner than Luskan worth the lives of every person on that ship?"

"Yes." Perrault said without turning around to face me.

I let my hands fall to my sides. "But why?" My voice was choked with unshed tears and I could barely push out the words.

"Because Asbeel has eyes everywhere. The demon was wounded, surely, but not badly. He will not stop looking for you, so we must step quickly to keep you out of sight. We cannot remain still, the way we were on the ship."

I shook my head. "But a ship is not still. It's always moving. That makes no sense."

Perrault stomped his foot hard, his boot cracking sharply against the floor. "I tell you where we're going, and there we will go, and that is the end of it. I know how to keep you safe. You do not."

My tears had dried, and I was just angry. "Why is that so important? Is my life more important than the sailors'? More important than Joen's?"

"It is to me!" Perrault swung around from his seat on the bed and glared at me. I could see what he'd been hiding. His silk shirt was soaked with blood, from the top of his wounded shoulder all the way to his waist.

The sight caught me off guard, and left me breathless. A million questions spun in my head then disappeared. I wanted to respond, to say something, anything, but no words came out. Perrault continued.

"A lesson for you, *child*,"—he spat the word angrily, as if it were an insult—"the most important one you shall ever hear from me. You protect first those you love then yourself, and last everyone else. You are my ward, so I will protect you first among all the souls in this world. And if doing so means harming others, even those who deserve no such harm, then so be it."

R.A. & Geno Salvatore

He grimaced then turned his back to me, pulling off the shirt and the bandage beneath. I saw the wound only for an instant, but it was long enough to horrify me.

The gash was an angry red, dripping watery, pale fluid. The flesh around it was blackened and burned where the demon's fire had touched it. It looked as if it had not healed at all—it looked as if it had grown worse.

Perrault got up and opened the cupboards. Finding what he sought, he pulled out a fresh linen sheet. He murmured a few words, poured some liquid on the fabric from a vial in his pocket, and tore the sheet into strips. Quickly, sure-handedly, he wrapped the linen tightly around his torso then pulled a fresh shirt from the cupboard and put it on.

"It's not about me—is it?" My words came out in a rush. "None of this is about me. It's about this stone. If you really cared about me, you wouldn't have cursed me with it." I ripped my shirt open and tugged the bandolier off my chest. "Why don't you just take it back?"

I marched over to Perrault, shaking the leather strap with every step I took. "Because of this stone, I'm an orphan. Because of this stone, I don't even know my real name. So tell me, why is it worth so much to everyone? To everyone but me?"

Perrault turned to face me and I could see the pain in his sunken eyes. His beard seemed more white than gray; his pale skin sagged.

"That stone is your heirloom and it will be forever intertwined with your destiny. I cannot answer any more than that, Maimun. There are some things you must learn for yourself." He looked as if he'd aged a decade in the past hour. His breath was labored. "Now please, child, help me to the bed."

I took his hand and was shocked by how cold it felt. He shuffled to the bed and helped him slide beneath the woolen blanket.

"We will make port in three days," Perrault said. "From Waterdeep, we make for Silverymoon with all haste. I've a friend there who will hide you."

"But what of you?" I asked. "You're hurt. You need help."

R.A. & Geno Salvatore

"I'll be fine. And besides, the finest healers in all Faerûn are in Silverymoon. Now, get some rest."

I supposed the plan was as good as any, though I knew the journey to Silverymoon would be long. Perrault had just placed a salve and fresh bandages on his wound, and he was a skilled healer. The oil he poured on the linen was surely magical, so I hoped the wound would heal soon.

I pulled some blankets from the cupboard, wrapped myself in them, and lay on the floor, affording Perrault the comfort of the cabin's only bed.

Perrault spent the next day in the cabin, barely moving, and sent me to fetch our meals. I had planned to seek out the captured crew, to learn Joen's fate, but Perrault's condition seemed far more urgent and I had to push my plan aside.

The second morning, he couldn't even rise from bed. The ship's healer came to see him, but was unable to do more than simply change the bandage. Captain Baram personally delivered our meals, to check on Perrault, and he informed us—informed me, as Perrault was asleep—that we were making fine time and were near the coast, but a powerful storm was battering Waterdeep and we couldn't sail into the harbor.

The third morning, Perrault did not wake.

Chapter Twenty-Three

"You should wait till we hit port." Captain Baram's voice was gentler than I'd ever heard it, full of something like pity. Somehow, that made me angry.

"Can't wait. Can't stay here with pirates," I spat.

We stood on the deck of the pirate ship mere moments after I had tried—and failed—to wake Perrault. I knew right away that we couldn't stay aboard and wait out the storm. Perrault didn't have that kind of time.

"Plenty of good healers in Waterdeep," Baram continued. "They'll fix him up right. You won't make it to Silverymoon."

I hefted Haze's saddle onto her back. "Best healers in Faerûn are in Silverymoon. Perrault said so."

Baram gave Haze a long look. "You sure she'll make it to shore?"

"She wouldn't let Perrault down. No chance, not ever." I finished with the saddle buckles and moved to Perrault, who lay on a cot the crew had dragged onto the deck. "Help me, would you?" I said, and a pair of crewmen obliged, helping me hoist him onto the saddle. His skin was hot and feverish, and his eyes flickered but never fully opened. He seemed halfway between sleep and waking, halfway between life and death.

I began to tie Perrault into the saddle.

"You'll be riding straight into a thunderstorm," the captain said. "Storm this far north, this time of year, gonna be a rough one, I'll tell you that much."

R.A. & Geno Salvatore

"We'll make it." I took Perrault's cloak from his back and fastened it around my neck. It was too long and dragged on the ground, but I didn't care. I reached into his boot sheath and withdrew his magical stiletto, sliding it into one of my belt loops. I slipped the straps of our haversack over my shoulders. Though it contained hundreds of books, it felt light as a feather.

"I have no doubt you'll make it," Baram said. "But you must make haste, or he will not."

I nodded, and swung up into the saddle. "I thank you for your hospitality, Captain Baram," I said, holding out my hand.

He took it in his strong grasp, and gave a firm shake. "If ever you find yourself in Luskan, do come find me," he said.

I gave him one last nod, took up Haze's reins, and headed overboard.

I had no plan to travel to Silverymoon, nor to trust Perrault's fate to the healers in Waterdeep,

The Stowaway

but I wasn't about to confide my real destination to a pirate.

I knew the one who could save Perrault, and she lived in Baldur's Gate.

Baldur's Gate, where I had been only a few days ago.

Baldur's Gate, the city where Perrault had been wounded trying to protect me.

We ran southeast, covering a great distance in a short time. After a few hours, the coast was in sight—and not a moment too soon, as I could feel Haze growing weary beneath me. At first, it had felt as if she were running on a cloud, but her hooves soon began to splash the water with every stride. We would be ashore soon, but along the coastline loomed a massive black cloud. Lightning rent the air, and waves of thunder rolled out to greet us like some ominous warning.

Turn back, said the thunderstorm. *It is futile. You are doomed. Turn back.*

Soon we were riding through a downpour, bolts of lightning crackling overhead, thunder following close behind. The storm increased in

R.A. & Geno Salvatore

fury as bolt after bolt blazed out, the thunder chasing it like an evil laugh, the world laughing in my face, taunting me.

But we made the shore.

Haze stumbled and nearly fell as her hooves finally touched solid ground. Tired and soaked, I tumbled head-over-heels off her back, landing hard. Perrault remained firmly tied in place. His breathing was exceedingly shallow, and the bandage over his wound was saturated.

I climbed to my feet and walked to Haze, laying my face against hers. Those intelligent gray eyes looked at me, exhausted.

"I know you're tired," I said to her, "but if we stop now, he dies."

I could see in the way she reacted that she understood me. She pulled herself up, forced her back straight, and stood with pride, power, and grace.

"That's my good girl," I whispered, pulling myself back into the saddle. Haze was off and running before I even settled into my seat.

A normal horse moving at a normal pace can

cover about fifty miles in a day if the weather is good and her rider lets her run. The journey from Waterdeep to Baldur's Gate is about five hundred miles, so the journey should have taken about ten days.

We made it in two.

We thundered through the city gates at a full gallop, Haze still managing a run despite having not slept, not even stopped her run, in forty hours and five hundred miles. The city guards shouted in protest and tried to stop us, but they couldn't keep up. Soon we were pounding through the city streets. Haze knew our destination without my guidance, and finally we skidded to a halt in front of the Empty Flagon.

Alviss, who had seen us coming, met us at the door.

I swung off the horse and handed her reins to the dwarf. "Take care of them," I said, turning to leave.

"Where are you going?" he asked.

"I must find Jaide. Where is she?"

"She's . . . she's in her temple," he stammered.

"But you shouldn't be here. The demon is still looking for you!"

"I don't care. I need to find Jaide, to save Perrault," I said. "Which temple is hers?"

"The Lady's Hall," he said. "But wait! Don't go just yet." Alviss ran through the Empty Flagon's door and returned a few seconds later, sweat beading on his brow. He motioned for me to hold out my hand, and into my palm he pressed a slip of parchment. "You'll need this. Read the word aloud and she'll know it's you. It's the only way to enter her temple."

I was running toward the temple district before he could say another word. I heard him yelling after me, a stream of words lost to the wind, but his last two broke through clearly enough: "Be careful!"

Chapter Twenty~Four

The Lady's Hall—the temple to Tymora, goddess of good fortune and a matron deity to Baldur's Gate—was like nothing I had ever seen. It was huge and magnificent. High walls of white stone had statues placed every few feet depicting the goddess Tymora, her sister Beshaba, or one of her heroes fighting some dragon or devil. Mighty towers rose all around the building. Carvings covered them, layer upon layer of reliefs winding up the walls. Each tower was a giant work of art. At their tops were bells, perfect in both shape and sound.

I didn't stop to stare at the massive building. I had a purpose, and I moved deliberately, circling the temple to the east. I came to a narrow alley between the temple and another large building—it looked like a wealthy person's home—and moved along, looking for the door. But I found no entrance on either of the structures.

Behind the large house I found a ramshackle, run-down hut. The hovel's weather-beaten door had a carving of a sun with a face on it, eyes closed and mouth slightly upturned.

I reached into my pocket for the parchment and when I pulled it out there was another object in my hand. I unfolded the parchment, intent upon reading the word and entering the place.

"Took you long enough."

I started, because I recognized that voice.

Asbeel.

"At last you have come to fulfill your destiny. And you brought me the key to the priestess's home. Well done!" He laughed a terrible laugh.

I crumpled up the paper with my left hand and slipped it into a pocket, reaching with my

R.A. & Geno Salvatore

right for the stiletto on my belt. I tried to keep my hand steady, but the unfamiliar weight of the stiletto and the cold feeling in my gut made that impossible.

"Begone, snake," I hissed at him.

When I drew the weapon, Asbeel laughed even louder than before.

"The bard's cloak, and his dagger too! The rumors must be true—mighty Perrault is dead!"

He was defenseless; he had no weapon, not even his obsidian staff. His eyes were half-closed as he laughed. I snapped my wrist—the stiletto lengthened into a fine saber—and leaped at him, lunging for his throat.

But my sword passed harmlessly though him.

I knew my mistake as soon as I heard the beat of wings behind me. The illusion in front of me faded as I spun to face the real Asbeel, swooping down from the rooftops, his obsidian staff swinging for my head. I barely managed to get my sword up to block, but the strength of the blow was incredible. I went flying backward, the sword falling from my hand, and landed hard.

The Stowaway

"No more games, little one. You were mine from your birth, and with the bard gone, I claim you for my own. As it should be. Do not resist, or I will have to hurt you." He stalked forward, staff at the ready.

I had seen Asbeel fight Perrault and I knew I couldn't hope to defeat the demon. I got to my feet and retrieved my sword, quickly thinking through my options. What could I do? What could I use against him?

Then there was a blinding flash that set the world alight; and there was a voice, a woman's voice, cool and velvety and powerful all at once.

"Let him be, demon, he is beyond you," said the voice. "Come and play with me a while." Somewhere I heard a door click shut. The light was suddenly gone, and standing in the alley was the beautiful Jaide.

She was unarmed and unarmored, but still she looked formidable. Asbeel sensed it too. He turned from me, dropping his staff and drawing his sword. The blade burst into flame as he rushed her. A staff appeared in her hand, not a physical

R.A. & Geno Salvatore

object but a concentrated beam of light, and she parried his blow and struck back hard.

Asbeel barely managed to dodge, and he fell back a step. Jaide pressed the attack, her every movement graceful, the staff an extension of her will. The fight was dazzling, but it could not hold my focus, for suddenly a voice spoke in my head.

Run away, Maimun, Jaide said without speaking. *Run and hide.*

Perrault is sick! I mentally screamed back, somehow knowing she would hear me. *You need to help him!*

I have always helped him. But there is nothing more either of us can do for him now except to keep you and the stone safe. There was a finality to her words, but also serenity. I felt my heart clutch in my chest at the confirmation that Perrault was truly gone.

I don't want the stone, I replied.

That's not your choice to make. Keep it, and keep it safe.

Where should I go? I thought, defeated.

Anywhere but here. It is best if I do not know. Don't let the city guards see you, if you can, for many of them are allied with your foes. Run now, and take heart, for you will be blessed with luck in whatever travels you take.

I nodded at her, though she could not see—the battle raged on, sword and staff clashing together, bursts of fire and light illuminating the shadowy alley. I turned and ran.

I stopped at the end of the alley, one final thought coming to mind, and I hoped she could still hear me. *Will you kill Asbeel?*

Her response was faint, so faint at first I couldn't understand it. But she repeated it over and over, or perhaps it was merely an echo: *That is for you to do.*

R.A. & Geno Salvatore

Part Three

The Stowaway

A sharp bang on the door startled me from my tale. "Grub's up, Cap'n," came the muffled call from outside.

"Good, good. Bring mine in here," the pirate sitting before me replied. He paused a moment. "Make that a double ration."

No response came from outside save heavy booted footsteps walking away.

"So you're the captain then?" I asked. "That's new."

"What, ye think we'd let any old salt interrogate ye?"

"Is that what you've been doing?"

"Somethin' like that. Found out who ye sailed with, didn't I?"

"You found out who I sailed with long ago," I said.

Again the knock, and the door swung open, revealing a sandy passage leading to . . . was that the night sky? The rhythmic pounding of the waves against a cliff drifted up the corridor, along with the smell of salt water. A flicker of light at the end of the hall told me there was probably a campfire, and there was a low hum, like a song being sung in the distance. The other pirates were nearby.

I pondered the possibility of escape—bowl over the captain, maybe take his sword, and fight my way past this other pirate whose hands were full. But that would put me outside, among the whole crew. Their mooring would surely be someplace hidden, a cove or an island. There would be nowhere for me to run.

No, I decided it wasn't the time for an escape. Perhaps when the captain left.

Once the captain had his food, the door swung shut again.

"Thinkin' it, weren't ye?" he asked.

"I don't know what you mean."

"Ye were gonna make a run fer it."

I shrugged. "It wasn't my moment."

"No, it weren't. Ye think yer moment'll come soon, do ye?"

"I've been through worse than this."

The captain set down his food—a lump

R.A. & Geno Salvatore

of some shapeless slop and two small cuts of blackened, salted meat—and began picking at it.

"Hungry, are you?" I asked.

"You bet yer ugly arse I'm hungry. Captainin' be hard work."

"Hence the double rations."

"What, did ye think some of it was fer ye? Ye don't get food till I says ye get food."

I shrugged. "Then you get no more of my story."

The captain stopped. "Ye finished yer story, didn't ye? Ye already told me what happens next. Ye ran off from the demon, found Deudermont's ship, and stowed away. Ye met the drow, fought the sea troll, and made good with yer captain who offered ye a job aboard his ship. Got back to where ye started from."

"I did, but there's still more to tell."

"Yar, I know. Let me tell it. Ye sailed with Deudermont fer the next six years and then ye got yerself caught by me crew. Good

229

tale. Not worth me giving ye any o' me food."
Some of the colorless slop spilled from his
mouth with each word.

"If you believed that, you wouldn't have
taken your meal here."

The pirate stared at me for a long while.
"Clever boy, ain't ye?" He reached down,
took one of the slices of meat, and tossed it
to me. "Speak, then."

I took a bite. It wasn't half bad, despite
its appearance, and I was famished.

"Very well," I began. "Let's pick up back
on *Sea Sprite.*"

R.A. & Geno Salvatore

Chapter Twenty–Five

Sea Sprite had no empty cabin to house the several sailors wounded in the skirmish with the pirates. Instead, Captain Deudermont had a spare sail hung wall-to-wall in the crew cabin, separating the dozen bunks nearest the stern of the ship.

Deudermont said that would prevent dirt and diseases from the other sailors from creeping into the same area as the wounded and causing infection. I figured it was to keep the garish injuries, some much worse than my own gash, out of sight of the rest of the crew.

I was given the bunk closest to the port side of the ship, directly beneath a small porthole. As the ship sailed south, my porthole faced directly into the sunrise, and I took advantage of it on the second morning after the battle. The porthole was too high to see out of without standing on my cot, and I still felt lightheaded, but I hauled myself up and stared out at the brightening sky.

From my low vantage point, the horizon was an unbroken stretch of water. The rising sun appeared, slowly at first, then growing, until it filled my view, the brilliant light blinding me.

I thought of Perrault, of the first sunrise I had watched with him those many years ago. A new beginning, he had called it. A new day. Was this the same? Could I begin anew, right now, right here?

No, I decided, I could not. A weight still hung around my neck, and I couldn't start over as long as I carried it.

I was so wrapped up in my thoughts that I didn't notice the laughter behind me. It was more wheeze than laugh, filled with phlegm and more than likely some blood. Only when the laugh

R.A. & Geno Salvatore

turned into a hacking cough did I take note.

I turned to face a wounded sailor. He wasn't too old, but his face was worn, wrinkled, and leathery. I didn't see his wound at first—he was covered foot to neck by a blanket, and heaving with that awful cough—but when I saw it, my stomach turned. His left leg was missing from the knee down, and from the bloodstains on the sheets, it had been freshly amputated.

Gradually his cough subsided and the man was peaceful, but lathered in sweat. I knew that if I were to touch him, his flesh would be burning but that sweat would be cold. His cheeks were pale, his muscles slack. But his eyes were bright, staring at me.

"Are you all right?" I asked him. Only when he started laughing again did I realize how foolish the question was—he had lost his leg, and from the sound of that cough, he was seriously ill.

This time, the laugh didn't turn into a cough. Instead, it turned into words. "All right? I suppose I am, then. I didn't expect to see another sunrise at all, but there she is! 'Course, there's a boy blocking my view, but that don't bother me so much. He isn't hogging all the light." His voice, like his laugh, was choked with phlegm. He had the sound of a dying man, and my stomach dropped at the thought.

I flushed red and sat down on my cot. "Sorry, sir," I said. "I didn't realize you were awake."

"That's all right, kid," he replied. "But my name ain't sir—it's Tasso—and I'd much prefer if ye called me by it."

I nodded slowly. "I'm Maimun," I told him.

"You ever watch a man die, Maimun?" he asked. I heard no fear in his voice, only curiosity. "And I don't mean, have y'ever seen a man cut down by a sword. That's one thing, and it's horrible, but it ain't the same as watching a man die. I want to know—have you ever been near a man who could talk to you one moment, and the next he's gone?"

I started to shake my head, to say no, I hadn't ever seen that, but I stopped myself, thinking of Perrault. One day he was talking, trying to lead me to safety. The next day, he was asleep and I'd never hear his voice again.

"Is that a yes or a no?" Tasso asked.

I quickly shook my head. I knew where his questions were leading—Tasso was telling me that he was dying. And as much as I wanted to keep the truth about Perrault from myself, somehow I couldn't bring myself to hold back the truth from a man who was not long for the world. It didn't seem right that the last conversation he would ever have should be soiled with a lie, or even a half-lie.

"I've seen a man dying." A lump rose in my throat. "But I've never seen a man die."

"If ye don't think ye can handle it, you probably should get out of here soon," he said. Already his voice was lower, quieter than it had been, as if the energy of the conversation was draining him. "I was supposed to go east," he continued. "Supposed to follow my family out there, past the Sea of Falling Stars. Promised 'em I'd come find 'em."

"Why didn't you?"

"Never had the time."

I blinked a few times, remembering what Perrault had once told me about time.

"How old are ye, Maimun?" Tasso asked.

"Twelve, sir. Er, twelve, Tasso."

The Stowaway

He wheezed out a laugh. "Same age I was when I first took to the seas. Been on the ocean twenty years, been in the world thirty-two. I had plenty of time, didn't I? But I ne'er made it to the east."

"It isn't about how much time you have, it's about how much time you have to spare," I said quietly.

He looked at me for a long while. "Now ain't them just the wisest words I've ever heard?" He reached out and grasped my arm, pulling me toward his face. I felt his hot breath on my cheeks, but I was not revolted, I didn't try to pull away. "Time ain't spare, kid," he said, his voice low and choked. "Ye don't get given yer time, ye make it for yerself. Ye've got twenty years to catch me. Don't let it slip, waiting for something. Go east."

He let go and fell back onto his cot, his breathing shallow and labored. He sounded as if he was in pain, as if the air burned his lungs and throat as he gulped down his breaths. But a look of peace stole over his face, a serenity in his expression that I had not seen before.

R.A. & Geno Salvatore

I took his hand and held it. His breaths grew less frequent, and quieter, until I had to put my face close to his to hear it at all.

Less than an hour after he introduced himself to me, I held the hand of the sailor Tasso and watched his very last breath leave his body.

I sat on the edge of my cot, holding Tasso's hand even as it grew cool, for a very long time. The sun had risen beyond my porthole view, the diffuse light in the dusty cabin giving it an eerie feel. I sat there, holding the dead sailor's hand, imagining it was Perrault.

Only a few days earlier, I had raced to Baldur's Gate with Perrault, determined to find a way to save him. When I had the chance to say one last good-bye, right before I headed to the wharf to stow away on this very ship, I had passed it by. I had told myself that he would be better off without me, that the danger from Asbeel was too great. But I knew that wasn't true.

Perrault had raised me for six years, had dedicated his life to my protection. He had taught me, had shown me the world. He was wounded in my

The Stowaway

defense, had died to protect me. He was the only family I'd ever known. And I hadn't had the courage to be there, holding his hand as he slipped into the next world.

What had he felt, I wondered, when he died. Had his face worn the same look of peace that Tasso's had? Had he perhaps awakened, seeking to speak to me, if only for a moment, to admit he was done and would soon be gone?

Who had held Perrault's hand when he died?

The ship's healer arrived to find me holding the dead man's hand and weeping softly. He gently separated my hand from Tasso's and helped me back to my cot.

I barely heard him as he talked to me, and to the two crewmen he'd brought with him. Tasso had died because his wounds were infected, and to leave him would risk infection for the other wounded. He would be removed, and would be buried at sea that very day—that is, he would be wrapped in cloth, tied to a plank, weighted with stones, and released overboard.

Would I be buried at sea if my wound became

R.A. & Geno Salvatore

infected and I died? I had no ties to these sailors. Would they care if I disappeared? If I died? Would anyone?

I fell back onto my hard cot and wept, crying alternately for Perrault, for Tasso, and for myself, the orphan boy, wounded and wandering, with no roots or home to call my own.

"Self-pity does not become you." The voice caught me off guard. It was quiet and gentle, but full of strength. I looked up to see a black hand pulling back the corner of the canvas separating the makeshift infirmary, and a pair of violet eyes staring at me from beneath the raised corner.

"It wasn't self-pity," I lied, indignant. "I was crying for Tasso." I motioned to the empty cot.

"You barely knew Tasso. You were crying for yourself."

"You barely know me."

The dark elf Drizzt nodded his assent. It was true, of course, that we barely knew each other. But looking into his eyes, I felt again the bond I had sensed when I first saw him. I felt again that I had known him all my life. And I was sure he knew it, and I hoped he felt the same connection.

"You're right. I wasn't crying for Tasso. I was crying for someone else, but it wasn't for me."

"Why do you cry for this other person?"

"Because he's dead!" I practically screamed.

Drizzt nodded. "Of course," he said. "But why do you cry for the dead?"

I stuttered a few times before I could answer. "Because he's gone and he won't come back."

"But where has he gone?"

"I don't know. Tymora's realm in Brightwater, I suppose. He's gone to be with his goddess."

"If you believe that, then why cry for him? If he is in a good place, shouldn't you be happy for him?"

"I . . . I don't know."

"Look inside. You were crying because you lost him, not because he is lost. You were crying because this world is suddenly less full than it was before. And that is a fine reason to grieve. But be aware of that fact. You were crying for yourself."

I stared at him for a long time, at that dark elf

R.A. & Geno Salvatore

so full of wisdom. He knew things, many things, I realized. He knew the truth about me before even I knew it.

"When a sailor dies, why do they bury him at sea?" I asked, trying to hold back tears.

"People are always buried near their families," Drizzt said. "So when a sailor dies, his family at sea will always be nearby."

"What do you mean, his family at sea? Do sailors take their parents or their children out on the water with them?"

"Sometimes. But I meant the others on his crew." Drizzt stepped into the room and sat beside me on my cot. "There are all kinds of family, as you shall learn. Every sailor on this ship is brother or sister to every other. Now, enough of this discussion. How is your arm?"

I hesitated for a moment before I realized what he was talking about. Unconsciously, I started moving my left arm in circles. "The pain is gone," I said, "but it feels . . . tight."

Drizzt nodded. "Can you stand? Can you walk?"

The Stowaway

I shrugged. "I can stand. Haven't tried walking."

"Do." He offered me his arm, which I accepted and used to pull myself up off the cot.

I stood unsteadily for a moment. "I feel a bit woozy," I said. "But I think I'm all right."

"Good. The captain wants to see you." He handed me a small sack, which I opened to find a fresh outfit, complete with a clean shirt, a leather belt with a sheath for my stiletto, and a worn pair of boots. And the leather sash holding the magical stone.

I looked up to see the flap of the canvas fall behind the departing drow. "Drizzt!" I called after him. My chest hurt from the effort of the shout, but the flap lifted and the dark elf reappeared.

"Forget something?" he asked.

"If I die, where will they bury me? I have no family."

He looked at me for a moment. "You have a family. You just don't know it yet."

Chapter Twenty-Six

"What do you know of the sea?" Captain Deudermont asked me.

"The ocean is vast and unknown, stretching away from the western coast of Faerûn forever, to unknown tracts of water and perhaps land," I recited. "It serves as a means of conveyance between the points along the coast, much faster than travel by land, though often more dangerous. The first . . ."

Captain Deudermont stopped me with an upraised hand. "You have read Volo," he said.

"Yes sir."

"That is good. But what do you know of the sea that is practical?"

I paused for a moment. "I don't know what is practical at sea," I answered truthfully.

"Have you ever been aboard a ship before?"

"Just once." I winced at the memory, and Deudermont noticed.

"You didn't enjoy the experience?"

Again I hesitated. How could I explain the events of my previous sea voyage? Of course, one word would fully and accurately describe my troubles. "Pirates, sir."

Deudermont nodded. "So twice you have been to sea, and twice your ship has been attacked. You have some terrible luck, Maimun."

"Apparently so, sir."

"Back when you were at sea before, what did you do?"

"I spent most of my time in the gull's . . . I mean, the crow's nest, sir." Deudermont perked up at that.

"Did you have the eyes for it?" he asked.

R.A. & Geno Salvatore

"Could you make out objects on the horizon?"

I nodded. I had seen the ship Joen had pointed out. I had even seen a ship at night, that horrible night, and I told him so.

"That is impressive. It usually takes a sailor months, even years, to attune his eyes to the tricks of the light on the open ocean."

"I was only at sea for short time, sir."

Deudermont smiled. "Your manner and honesty have confirmed my choice for you. Your position on the ship will be as my cabin boy. Your tasks will be mostly menial. While at sea, you will run orders to the crew, and you will bring meals to me. You will maintain the cabinets where the captain's log and the charts are kept." He motioned to a large piece of furniture I had assumed was a cupboard. "When we're in port, you'll watch the ship if I go ashore. In exchange for all these tasks, you'll be paid a modest wage in silver, and you'll also be paid in knowledge. You'll learn, from the crew me, all forms of seamanship—tying knots, navigating by the stars—"

"Oh! I know how to . . ." I blurted out the

words before I realized how rude my interruption was. Captain Deudermont's gaze was stern, and I flushed bright red.

"Where did you learn to navigate?"

"I read it in a book."

"There's a big difference between a book and the real thing."

I shook my head. "When I was traveling with . . . my father, he wouldn't tell me where we were, so I'd use the stars to figure it out," I answered. "There isn't any difference between starfinding on land and on sea, is there?"

Deudermont's expression softened a bit. He looked almost curious. "It is easier, in fact, at sea, since the horizon is flatter. My young man, I think you have a remarkable mind. Here is your first task. Run these orders to the guards at the brig, where the pirates are being held."

I was beaming at the compliment as I bounced out of the room, across the deck, down into the hold, and toward the brig.

Like any seafaring vessel, the ship was fitted with a simple prison, a single cell made of iron bars. The cell had no window and only one door, which was securely locked from the outside. The brig was large, but full. Two dozen pirates sat on the floor, packed as tightly as they could fit. Two of *Sea Sprite*'s sailors stood guard, leaning against the wall beside the cage. One of them absently twirled a ring of keys around his finger. The other appeared to be dozing, his chin resting on his chest and his shoulders slumped. Neither took any notice of my approach.

"Orders from Captain Deudermont," I said meekly. The guard with the keys jumped and nearly dropped them. The other didn't even stir.

"Oh, so the Cap'n's got you runnin' orders to pay your debt, does he?" he said, his voice loud and rough. It awoke his companion, who had been asleep on his feet. Startled awake, he jumped forward, his body moving too quickly for his legs. His feet tangled and down he went, landing with a heavy crash.

In the blink of an eye, the guard was back on his feet, brushing himself off and waving his fist at the caged pirates, who were laughing at him.

The Stowaway

One man, standing against the bulkhead at the back of the cell, wasn't laughing, though, or even smiling. He was short and thin, with a wide nose and too-small eyes. His skin appeared a pale blue, and his hair was the bluish white of a breaking wave. He was just staring—at me. Suddenly I felt very uncomfortable.

"Well then, hand them over," said the guard with the keys. I obliged, passing him the note, which he unfurled and scanned quickly.

"Oy, Tin, you're relieved," he said, looking at the other man. The clumsy sailor nodded and left without saying a word.

"His name is Tin?" I asked.

"Oh, no, his name's Tonnid. But we call him Tin-head , 'cause he's got as much brains in that skull as an empty tin cup. And I'm called Lucky, 'cause, well, I'm the luckiest salt you'll ever meet. What's your name?"

"My name is Maimun. It means 'twice lucky'."

Lucky broke out laughing. "Twice lucky, eh? But you're half my size!"

I joined in the laugh for a moment then looked

R.A. & Geno Salvatore

around. "So, if he's relieved, who's relieving him? Or does it say you have to guard alone?"

"Naw, naw, I ain't guarding this lot alone. You're supposed to fetch his replacement. Guy named Drizzitz." He cackled, and I knew he was directing it at me, though I didn't know why. "You're the stowaway ain't ya? Paying back the Cap'n for stealing his food by running these orders?"

"Yes, and no," I answered. "I stowed away, but the captain offered me a place on the crew."

In the blink of an eye, Lucky's mirth was gone. "Offered you a job? For stowing away and hiding through the fight? That don't seem half right. No it don't."

"I didn't hide. I fought. Got wounded, too!" I reached to the neckline of my shirt, intending to show him my scar. But that pirate who had been staring at me seemed to perk up as I reached, and I realized that to show him the wound would also reveal my leather sash. I hesitated.

"Well, then, let's have it, eh? Show me your wound, else I'll know you for a liar."

The Stowaway

Thinking quickly, I reached out and grabbed his hand, pulling it toward my chest. "Feel that?" I asked, putting his hand on my shoulder where the scar began. "You feel the wound?"

By the look on his face—a mix of horror and sympathy—I knew he felt it, the raised welt where the gash had been. "Ye got tarred," he said, low. "That's one of the things I been lucky about. Been sailing some thirty years and I ain't never got a wound so deep it needed the tar. You have me apologies, boy. But I didn't see you in the fight. Ya mind telling me what happened?"

Again I hesitated. How could I tell him about the fight, about the troll that had come looking for me? How could I tell him without revealing the artifact strapped to my chest—which the pirate in the brig seemed interested in. Worse, how would Lucky react if he deduced, as I had, that the pirates had attacked *Sea Sprite* because they were looking for me?

I couldn't tell him. I would have to lie.

"A pirate got into the hold where I was hiding," I began. Lucky immediately looked suspicious. I

R.A. & Geno Salvatore

figured he'd been on the deck, and he knew no pirate had entered the hold that way. Time to improvise. "He climbed up the stern. Had a big axe. You know that big hole in the aft hull? That's his doing—cut his way in."

"Must've been one big pirate to cut through the hull of a ship!" Lucky exclaimed.

"The biggest man I've ever seen," I replied. "I figure he had some orc—or something—in him. Anyway, so he chops into the hold right where I'm hiding. And he wants to go through the hold and up the hatch and attack the crew from behind. But I couldn't let him do that. So I sneaked up and tied a rope to his ankle then tied it to the rowboat and dropped the boat into the water."

"Oy, good thought! But how'd that get yourself a wound?"

"He crashed into me on his way out of the hold," I said. "Knocked me right into the splintered wood he'd cut through."

Lucky winced. "Guess you ain't as lucky as your name says, then."

"He's a liar." The voice caught me off guard. It

The Stowaway

was deep and powerful, but not harsh. It reminded me of the distant thunder of a storm on its way out, damage done but mercifully leaving. It belonged to the pirate in the back of the cage—only he was no longer at the back of the cage. He stood right against the bars, staring at me, unblinking.

"Oy, shut your mouth and don't talk no more, you wretched wretch!" Lucky drew his cutlass from its sheath and waved it threateningly at the man.

"The child is lying to you. He is concealing something."

Lucky spat at the pirate and stepped between us. "If ye think I'll trust you over the boy, you're dumber than a sea sponge."

"I don't ask for trust. But I have a question. Little Maimun, what is that lump in your shirt beside your heart?"

Lucky turned to look at me, staring intently. I was sure he'd see the lump and ask about it, and I couldn't answer him. I slowly moved my feet, one behind the other.

"I need to find Drizzt to relieve Tin," I said,

R.A. & Geno Salvatore

and before Lucky could say anything, I turned on my heel and sprinted away.

I found Drizzt on the deck at the prow of the ship. The disguise that made him appear as a sun elf was off, his black skin exposed to the summer sun. He held his head high, eyes closed against the breeze, feeling the sun on his face and the wind sweeping back his thick white hair. I crept up silently, not wanting to disturb his meditation, but he heard my approach.

"Greetings, Maimun," he said, not opening his eyes or turning his head. "Captain Deudermont told me of your new position. Congratulations."

"Thank you, sir," I said. "I have orders from the captain for you."

"To take my shift at the brig, I'm suppose," he said.

"Yes sir."

"Thank you, then." He opened his eyes and turned to face me.

The Stowaway

"Can I ask you a question?" I said.

"You just did."

"I mean . . . you know what I meant." I stammered, suddenly nervous. "Where . . . where is your home? Where is your family?"

He looked at me for a moment, studying me intently. I don't know what he was looking for, but apparently he found it. He nodded, and answered. "My home is wherever my family is, and my family are my friends and traveling companions. It is not a large family, so far, as few trust me. Few trust any of my dark heritage."

"But the others who fought the pirates here," I said. "Wulfgar, and the dwarf, and the woman. They trust you, right?"

"They do. And those three are my family. Well, those three and a fourth who is not here. You're an orphan, aren't you?"

"I am." I sighed. Thrice an orphan, I wanted to say. "How did you know?"

"You understand what I mean by family. Most do not. Most think of a family as parents and siblings, aunts and uncles, but really, a family are those

R.A. & Geno Salvatore

people you know here," he pointed to his head, "and trust here." He laid his hand over his heart.

I nodded my agreement. "So who is the last of your close family?"

"A halfling named Regis. He was taken from us and is being held prisoner in Calimport by a very powerful and evil man. For his sake, we sail south."

"Sounds dangerous. Are you sure he wishes you to save him?" I asked. I immediately thought I should have picked my words more carefully, but Drizzt didn't seem upset.

"How do you mean?" he asked. I think he knew exactly what I meant, but he was leading me on. Perrault did the same thing. He'd lead me on, knowing the answer, to force me to articulate it. Because, he'd say, only after I had spoken it would I truly understand what I meant.

"I mean," I began, "are you sure he isn't in a cell somewhere, scared to death that you and your family—his family—might try to rescue him but fail? That one of you might be killed for his sake?"

The Stowaway

Drizzt nodded again, his expression somewhere between grim and hopeful. "I am quite
certain he's thinking exactly that."

"Then why go?"

"Because he cares more for us than for himself.
We'd be terrible friends if we didn't return the
favor." With that, he bowed his head slightly then
stepped to the ladder to the hold.

"Drizzt!" I called after him. "If you die, where
should they bury you?"

"It doesn't matter. My friends will know where
to look for me."

Instinctively, my hand went to my heart—
because, of course, he meant his friends would
only need to look within. But in reaching for my
heart, my hand bumped against something else.
Something the size of a child's fist, held in a
leather pouch. The stone.

RA. & Geno Salvatore

Chapter Twenty-Seven

The next several days were a blur. I spent my
waking hours running around the ship delivering
small scrolls of parchment, or verbally passing
orders to the sailors who couldn't read. I ran
Deudermont's meals from the galley to his cabin,
and was rewarded with the privilege of dining with
him. During those hours, Deudermont, true to
his word, began to teach me the craft of seamanship, telling me of the tactics of running a ship—
when and how to set sail or make port, weather
signs, and all the things a captain should know.

When I was idle, I learned the practical art of sailing. I spent hours sitting on the deck watching the crew as they went about their affairs. I memorized the knots they tied. I watched them furl and unfurl the sails, and turn those sails to catch the wind. I listened to the calls from the helm, usually just numbers, to change our bearing. Soon I was confident I could have undertaken any job on the ship. For the first time in my life, I felt at home.

I learned most of the crewmen's names, and some snippets of their stories, but I kept to myself and they did the same. I was worried that I would have to tell my story again, to lie again. I was worried that Lucky, in particular, had pieced some of it together, and that I would be blamed for the pirate attack. But even Lucky was friendly toward me, and he never once asked about the lump on my chest.

The days flew by, and before I knew it, we were sailing into Memnon.

I thought Baldur's Gate to be a great city, but it would have fit a dozen times into the sprawl that was Memnon. As the northernmost port in

R.A. & Geno Salvatore

Calimshan, the city was built where the Calim Desert met the ocean, where the sea breeze could break up the stifling heat of the parched sandscape. The sprawl reminded me of the poorest parts of the lower city of Baldur's Gate mixed with the richest parts of the upper city, thrown into a mixing pot and stirred well. Ramshackle huts built of driftwood stood against mighty palaces of white marble. Low warehouses lined the docks, like in Baldur's Gate, but the windows were empty of glass, and by the sheer volume of people moving in and out, I figured most of the structures served as homes for those who could find nowhere else to be, rather than as storage for trade goods.

The sprawl made its way into the harbor as well. The docks were completely full, and a hundred more ships were anchored beyond them. Great trade galleons mingled with tiny fishing vessels, and the flags of a hundred ports of a dozen kingdoms flew from the masts.

Moving around the ships were longboats, each crewed by a dozen men chained to their seats and pulling at oars. Each boat bore a beacon lantern

The Stowaway

at the bow, and a flag flew from the stern, marking them as official vessels of the city of Memnon. Captain Deudermont informed me that they were the Memnon Harbor Guard, and they were searching incoming vessels for contraband. Or, more accurately, they were forcing those ships holding contraband to pay bribes. Otherwise, they would be refused access to the port.

They would also be the ones taking the captured pirates off our hands. A reward was offered for bringing captured pirates to Memnon. But Deudermont said the Harbor Guard would surely make up some reason the reward could not be paid. They were experts at extorting money, he said, but very bad at paying it. And they wouldn't be checking our ship for at least a day.

On the first day in port, Drizzt and his companions prepared to depart.

Drizzt talked to Captain Deudermont in his cabin, and I wasn't invited to sit in. I tried to listen at the door, but their voices were low and I couldn't make out what was said.

On the way out, Drizzt gave me a look. "I'll

R.A. & Geno Salvatore

see you again," the look said—and he put his hand over his heart in salute. His skin was as light as a sun elf's again, just as it had been the first time I'd laid eyes upon him. Though I knew it was an illusion, it was still strange to see him again in his magical disguise. At least he didn't look as uncomfortable as he had that first time. I felt a strange kinship as I watched him walk away. Something had changed for him aboard *Sea Sprite*, just as it had for me.

Drizzt and his friends boarded a hired launch, and he was gone, drifting through the harbor toward the docks. All I had left of him was that look.

I awoke the next morning to shouts coming from the deck. I quickly dressed and scurried above to discover three uniformed members of the Memnon Harbor Guard climbing aboard. Captain Deudermont rushed from his cabin to meet them. He looked somewhat disheveled,

The Stowaway

obviously surprised by the quick arrival of the inspectors. He'd told me to expect them late that day or early the next.

I quickly moved to his side. As soon as I reached him, he said, "Maimun, go rouse the crew. Tell them we're unloading the pirates."

I opened my mouth to say something, but Deudermont waved his hand at me and turned back to his conversation with the guards.

I did as I was told, and soon the pirates were marching up from the hold, each man tied at the wrists and ankles, and each tied to the man in front of and behind him. On the captured pirate vessel, a similar scene occurred, but I noticed many more pirates crossing the deck than the two dozen crossing ours. It seemed the pirate ship had a larger brig than *Sea Sprite.*

But the pirates on our ship were more intimidating. The strange pirate who had confronted me was on deck, and he stared right at me again. I turned to the nearest crewman—it happened to be Tin.

"What's that one's problem, Tonnid?" I asked

R.A. & Geno Salvatore

him, motioning toward the staring pirate.

"I dunno, bud. He's just rude, I think."

"Aren't all pirates rude?"

Tin paused, thinking over his answer. "Yep, I figure they is," he replied. "That one's just even ruder."

Tin smiled at his almost-joke, and I laughed a little. It wasn't funny, but Tin liked people laughing at his jokes.

In the blink of an eye, Tin's smile was gone, replaced by a look of shock and horror.

Behind me I heard a soft thud, followed by loud shouting. I turned to see the strange pirate free of his bonds, the ropes uncut but lying on the deck. The man charged right at me.

"Hey, you's gonna get it for that, mister ruder!" Tin shouted, jumping in front of me, fists up in front of his face, ready to throw a punch.

The blue-faced pirate didn't hesitate, and didn't flinch when Tin threw a heavy punch at his jaw. The blow landed with a crunch, the sound of bone breaking, I thought. But the pirate didn't even slow. Instead, Tin fell back a step, clutching his wounded hand. The pirate bowled right over him, shoving him roughly to the deck, and reached out for me.

My stiletto was out, thrusting for his hand. Like Tin's, my blow struck squarely, but had no effect, bouncing harmlessly aside. The hand grabbed the front of my shirt and I was airborne.

The pirate, with me in his grasp, took two running strides and leaped over the side of the ship. With a splash, we hit the water and plummeted to the bottom, as if we were tied to one of the ship's anchors.

I struggled against that iron grip, but he was strong and I couldn't break free. I swung my stiletto at him, but the water slowed my movements, and I felt as though I was striking stone. The pirate ignored me and ignored the water, walking along the floor of the harbor as if he were strolling down a sunny street.

I held my breath as long as I could, until I felt as though my lungs would explode. I hadn't had a chance to take a deep breath before we entered the water, and the exertion of swinging my dagger

R.A. & Geno Salvatore

used up my air. The pirate took no notice of my struggling. He walked along, uncaring that I was about to drown.

I could take it no more. My breath came out in a bubble, and I inhaled deeply.

But somehow, air, not water, entered my lungs.

The pirate finally acknowledged my existence. He pulled me in front of him, face to face. He looked at me as I took my first few unsettling breaths then he began to laugh.

"Fool," he said. His voice sounded even more sinister distorted by the water. "Did you think I would let you die? You are worth twice as much alive! Though truly, the sum for your corpse would still be worth my time." Again, that terrible laugh.

An old horror jolted through me. Only one person—one creature—would put a bounty on my head. The foul blue pirate meant to sell me to Asbeel.

That notion sent me into a frenzy. I tried with all my might to pull away. I stabbed at him,

The Stowaway

at his chest and his face, again and again. I kicked and screamed, though my words were so distorted as to be unintelligible. I fought desperately, but I only ripped my shirt, and as soon as that happened, the pirate adjusted his grip, holding firm to my wounded left shoulder.

And all the while, Memnon's docks approached.

The water in front of the pirate turned white. Not noticing, he continued walking—right into a thick sheet of ice.

At the instant of impact, I felt his grip loosen. I jerked sharply, bracing my feet against his thigh and pushing off with all my might, and I was free.

But in my next breath, I caught water, not air. I was choking, sputtering, with no air in my lungs and none to bring in. Instantly my chest ached, a horrible, acute pain, and I tried to resist the urge to breathe. The pirate reached for me, and I was tempted to grab his hand just so I could take a breath. But I knew if that hand caught me, I wouldn't be free again. I wanted to swim for the

R.A. & Geno Salvatore

surface, but the surface was a long way off, and I was weighed down by my sodden clothes. I would surely die before I made it.

Then I was rising, streaming through the water, and before I knew it I broke the surface—not just my head, but my entire body. I coughed and sputtered, and gulped down air and expelled water.

Glancing around to orient myself, I found I was much closer to the docks than to *Sea Sprite*. Somehow I was lying atop the water, floating perhaps an inch off the surface. A slight depression, like a bowl on the waves, formed beneath me, as if I repelled the water. Curious, I reached down to touch the surface, and some invisible force pushed back against my hand. I pushed harder, but it pushed harder back, the depression in the water growing deeper, my hand barely moving.

I looked up, wondering at the source of that miracle, and found it standing above me.

The man wore a deep blue robe and had a bearded face, which in turn wore an expression of pure amusement.

"Done coughing, boy?" he asked, his voice dripping sarcasm.

I nodded, taking a few more deep breaths to steady myself then stood bobbing in my invisible bowl. "Who are you, sir?" I asked.

He seemed pleased to be addressed as "sir," as if that was an uncommon occurrence. "My name is Robillard, and I work with the Memnon Harbor Guard. I was overseeing the transfer of Captain Pinochet and his pirates from *Sea Sprite* to our control, when that fool"—he motioned toward the water—"grabbed you. You're lucky to be alive, boy."

I shook my head. "He wasn't going to kill me, sir."

"Then what did he want with you?"

I hesitated. "It's personal," I finally said.

"You knew that pirate?" There was no sarcasm in his voice—he was accusing me.

"No, sir. He's working for someone who wants to capture me."

"So you're a runaway?" Robillard arched an eyebrow. "What is your name, child?"

R.A. & Geno Salvatore

I glared at him. "My name is none of your—"

Suddenly, the force that had kept me above the water gave way, and down I went with a splash. As soon as I was completely under, I was rising again. It happened so quickly that I landed perfectly on my feet, stunned but unhurt.

"Beware whom you speak to so rudely," Robillard said. "And more importantly, beware *when* you speak so rudely. Fool."

Another voice carried across the waves—a familiar voice. Lucky. "Oy, Maimun, you look all wet!" Then a friendly burst of laughter. "Not hurt, are ye?"

I turned to face the voice, and saw that *Sea Sprite* had already replaced her ruined launch. Lucky and two other crewmen glided toward me—Lucky standing at the prow, the other two rowing. They were still a good distance away, but would come alongside me quickly.

"No, I'm not hurt," I called. "How's Tin?"

"Broke his hand, he did. I always told him, never swing with a closed fist, you'll break it for sure, but did he listen? No sir, 'course not, he ain't smart enough to listen to me."

My mind spun in a dozen different directions as I watched the launch approach. Mostly my thoughts focused on Asbeel and his cohorts, on the troll I had thrown from the ship, and the strange pirate who had taken me captive. I had thought that out at sea, I would be safe from Asbeel. But I was wrong.

I had already caused the deaths of several men in the battle with the pirates—Tasso, and more whose names I didn't even know. I couldn't stand the thought of Deudermont, or Lucky, or Tin dying on my behalf. I couldn't allow it to happen again.

I turned to Robillard and asked, quietly so Lucky wouldn't hear, "How long will this enchantment last?" I motioned toward my feet.

"Hours, if I let it," he answered with a wink that was not unfriendly. "Why?"

"Hey, Lucky," I called, without breaking eye contact with Robillard. "Do me a favor."

"Whatsat?"

R.A. & Geno Salvatore

"Tell Captain Deudermont—thank you for your hospitality, and for your offer, but I am resigning my position aboard his ship."

I heard the oars stop rowing, and Lucky stuttered out something like, "What?"

Robillard looked at me hard then nodded and smiled. "So you *are* a runaway."

"A runaway." I almost laughed. "I guess you could say I've been running my entire life, sir."

And with that, I turned and sprinted across the water toward Memnon.

Chapter Twenty-Eight

Memnon's sprawl proved even more confusing on the ground than it had appeared from the ship. The streets weren't paved, and didn't seem to have been laid out according to any kind of plan. Instead, a street was simply any space not occupied by a building. The vast majority of the structures were shoddily built and atrocious to look at, but the people were amazing. As I pushed through the crowded streets, I saw that almost everyone was brightly dressed, their heads wrapped in turbans of red and blue and black. Most of their faces were covered by veils, some dark and obscuring, others sheer and showing a hint of the features beneath.

I moved with as much haste as I dared. I had no idea whether the city guard could be influenced by the demon. But I had learned that Asbeel's agents could be anywhere, and I couldn't risk attracting anyone's attention. I no longer had anyone to protect me—I no longer had anyone to fall on my behalf.

And how could I, in good conscience, associate with anyone ever again knowing a demon followed me? My heart sank as I pictured my future: a life of solitude, always moving, until one day I slipped and Asbeel caught up to me.

I considered leaving Memnon. I could head south, into the harsh Calim Desert. I had read books about survival in harsh climates, including the parched sandscape of the desert. I would be able to journey a few days into the desert, at least. Out there, out in the wasteland alone, I could bury the stone, and bury it deep. No one would follow me, and no one would find it. I would be free. And no one else would be hurt on my behalf.

But what would become of me then? Somehow the stone was linked to my family. Somehow it was part of my destiny. Perrault had told me so. How would he feel to know that I planned to toss it away? My face flushed at the thought and I knew the answer.

After all those days aboard *Sea Sprite*, I had learned one thing for certain: no matter how far I traveled, across the sea to the ends of Toril, through the sands of the Calim Desert, Asbeel would never be far behind. And I was so tired of running.

The streets of Memnon wound randomly and sometimes ended suddenly, but just as often met at the intersection of half a dozen streets, each looking exactly like the next. The sprawl was an enormous maze, and before long I was completely lost.

Just before sunset, I found myself somewhere in the middle of the city, with neither the outer walls nor the docks in sight, and no real idea where either might be. I couldn't wander around the city all night. Even if I wanted to leave Memnon, I had no idea how.

The Stowaway

Lost in thought, I turned down a darkened alley. My feet throbbed and my stomach ached with hunger. Soon I would have to find a place to rest.

A movement farther up the alley caught my eye, a shadow moving among the shadows.

In an instant, my pain flew away and my heart set to racing. Asbeel, or one of his dark agents, had come calling.

I turned back the way I came, and looked directly into a pair of glowing yellow eyes.

R.A. & Geno Salvatore

Chapter Twenty~Nine

Startled, I barely managed to stifle a scream as I backed up, reaching awkwardly for the stiletto sheathed in my belt. Just as my hand found the thin dagger's hilt, my heel found a crate, and already off my balance, I tumbled hard to my backside.

The yellow-eyed creature leaped in surprise at the sound, hissing and baring its feline claws at me, then darted into the shadows. I found myself laughing despite my situation. Defeated by a mere tabby cat!

I was left staring up at the sky, feeling ashamed that a tiny cat had so frightened me. I thought I heard footsteps clattering along the rooftop at the end of the dark alley.

Had Asbeel found me, even here? Or was I being paranoid?

I stared up at a pile of old crates, reaching nearly to the roof of the building. As I pulled myself to my feet, I thought of a phrase I had heard before—luck favors the bold.

It was time for me to be bold.

The crates proved easy to scale. The sturdy wood easily supported my weight and the pyramid shape of the stack formed almost a stairway. The topmost crate was barely three feet below the edge of the roof, and soon I was climbing out of the gloomy alley and into the glowing sunset.

Here the light was even brighter than it had been in the streets. The rooftops all around were made of some kind of white tile, and at that moment were perfectly angled to catch the rays of the descending sun. The glare stung my eyes. I

R.A. & Geno Salvatore

shaded my eyes and glanced back and forth across the glimmering rooftops.

I could see almost the entirety of Memnon laid out before me. At least I wouldn't be lost in the jumble of streets. I turned to the west and thought I saw a lanky, elf-like figure in a black and violet cloak slipping around the chimney of the rundown building.

I gripped my dagger tighter and took in a breath. If Asbeel wanted the stone, he would have to fight me for it. I would not let him chase me anymore.

I broke into a full run after the shadowy figure. Not three streets away, the figure seemed to slip down the side of the building and disappear. Even from a distance, I could see the stands of the marketplace below. They bustled with more people, I imagined, than lived in the entirety of Baldur's Gate. I had to hurry or I would lose him among the many people.

I leaped the last five-foot-wide alley onto the roof of a brick building. Directly below me, vendors' carts hustled down the street that led

The Stowaway

into the market square. The only question was how to make my way down from the rooftops back onto the street without anyone spotting me. It was perhaps twenty feet, a fair fall indeed. But I had read in one of Perrault's books that when falling beside a wall, martial warriors and monks of Shou Lung would use their hands and feet to slow their descent. Upon landing, they tuck and roll to absorb much of the momentum. It was a move I had longed to try since I'd first read about it and it seemed as good a time as any.

I tucked my dagger into my boot and dropped.

As I plummeted toward the ground, I realized that reading about a move and performing it were two very different things. With nothing to grasp at, I couldn't possibly slow myself. The surprised shouts of the people below barely registered. All I saw was the inevitable end of my journey, the unpaved dirt road, rushing up to meet me.

But then a pale form cut in front of me, a great white sheet of fabric, billowing in the breeze as it dangled from a clothesline. The sheet caught an unexpected gust of wind and fluttered toward me, a helping hand reaching out to catch me. I wasn't about to argue—I grabbed for the fabric.

The clothesline bowed and the sheet stretched, until finally the pins keeping the line and the fabric together surrendered to the force and popped loose, dropping me the last fifteen feet.

Instead of the hard-packed dirt road, I landed directly onto a cart of fresh melons. As I thumped down into the cart, melons exploded all around me, covering me, the laundry, and the street in red and purple juice and pulp.

"Oy, oaf! What've ye done?" A man rushed toward me, brandishing a gourd like a club. "I'll smack yer little head in, I will!"

I rolled out of the fruit cart and reached into my pocket. I pulled out what few coins I had and tossed them at the man. It was not nearly enough to pay for all the fruit, I knew, but it was something.

As the coins arced through the air, they caught the sun, distracting the man and the other onlookers long enough for me to turn and sprint down the road.

The Stowaway

The man continued to yell, though I couldn't make out the words, and a woman's shrill screech joined in. "He ruined my best bed sheet!"

I raced into the market and pushed through the crowd of people as best I could. Ahead of me I heard gasps, curses, and the crash of an overturned vendor's kiosk. It was Asbeel. It had to be. I couldn't let him hurt any more people on my behalf. I cut turn after turn, weaving around people's legs. At last I saw the figure dart into an alley, and I picked up my pace to follow him.

But as soon as I crossed into the shade of the narrow lane, I felt a little shiver roll through my body.

My heart pounded in my ears, but I was unable to move.

Chapter Thirty

"Don't fret, young Maimun," a voice said. A woman's voice, it was melodic and beautiful, and not at all threatening. "I have placed upon you a spell of holding. You will be unable to move for a short time. I am sorry for it, but it had to be done."

She stepped from the shadows, though it took me a moment to see her. She was completely covered in a dark robe, her hood pulled up, a black mask covering her face. The mask was a solid piece of obsidian, I figured, carved to look like a human face, completely blank of expression. It covered her whole face, even her eyes.

I tried to scream at her, to tell her to let me go, but I couldn't speak through her spell.

"Do you know what the stone you carry is, Maimun?" she asked. "It is an artifact blessed by the goddess Tymora, the bearer of good fortune. To the soul it has chosen, it will bring good luck, as long as it is close at hand."

And so I learned the answer I had wished so long for Perrault to give me, the power the stone held over me. The events of the past few moments fell into sharp focus. It was good fortune that I had found a billowing sheet to break my fall. And the melon wagon, coming at just the right moment— the stone had brought that good fortune upon me too. The pieces began to tumble into place, and they threw my whole journey, my whole life, into question. I had thought it was my choices that had led me to *Sea Sprite.* But had the stone itself given me the luck I needed to stow away unseen? Had it given me the strength to fight the troll, to save the ship? Without it, would I have ever found my place at sea?

R.A. & Geno Salvatore

"Unfortunately," the woman said as she crept closer, "luck in this world is finite. One person's good luck means another's misfortune."

The woman's objective became crystal clear, and I struggled mightily against her spell. My own purpose became clear.

For better or for worse, the stone had shaped my past and was meant to shape my future. I could not let it go. I could never let it go. The stone had been bestowed upon me for a reason. Perrault had trusted me to discover that reason and to protect the stone at all costs. After all that he had done for me, I couldn't betray his trust.

The woman calmly began opening my shirt. "This stone throws luck out of balance. While it favors you, it will hurt others. And that is not acceptable."

My shirt was open, and she reached around me to gently unfasten the buckle and remove the whole sash. I felt it pull away, as if my skin were stuck to the leather, as if my body stretched out, trying to hold onto it. But then it was gone. My chest stung where the stone had rested, and

The Stowaway

my heart felt empty.

She tucked the stone under her robe and stepped back. "The stone will be kept safe from those who seek to use it for ill gains, and you shall be free of your burden."

I had once dreamed of being free of the stone's burden. But now that it was gone, I realized how wrong I had been. This *hurt*.

"Now, Maimun, I'm going to cast another spell on you. This one will put you into a deep sleep. You'll wake up tomorrow morning, refreshed, and I urge you to look upon it as a new life."

I don't want a new life, I thought. I want the stone. I willed myself to reach for Perrault's dagger and for a moment, I thought I had broken her spell.

My voice broke through the silence. "Give . . . it . . . *back!*" I shouted.

But the woman began an arcane chant, and soon I found myself following along mentally. I drifted along the river of soothing sound she created and soon I was fast asleep.

R.A. & Geno Salvatore

※

The strange woman was wrong. I would not sleep until morning light. I woke up sometime long past darkness, to someone prodding at my shoulder.

I found myself staring at a pair of shiny leather boots. Rising from the boots was a pair of legs, clothed in fine black silk pants, and above that, a pristine white shirt.

And above that, a snarling, red-skinned elf face.

"Where is it, boy?" Asbeel spat at me. "Where is the stone?"

Find out what happens next!

Don't miss the next volume in the
Stone of Tymora trilogy coming
September 2009

About the Authors

R.A. Salvatore is the author of forty novels and more than a dozen *New York Times* best sellers, including *The Two Swords* which debuted at #4 on *The New York Times* best seller list.

Geno Salvatore has collaborated on several R.A. Salvatore projects including Fast Forward Games' *R.A. Salvatore's The DemonWars Campaign Setting* and *R.A. Salvatore's The DemonWars Player's Guide*. He co-authored R.A. Salvatore's DemonWars *Prologue*, a DemonWars short story that appeared in the comic book published by Devil's Due Publishing. He is a recent graduate of Boston University and lives in Massachusetts.